ECHOES OF DROWNING

LIS MCDERMOTT

This edition published in 2024 by Westwater Publishing

ISBN 978-1-7394507-4-8 (paperback 1st edition)
ISBN 978-1-7394507-3-1 (ebook 1st edition)

Dedicated to my great aunt and uncle, Amy and William Campbell,
survivor and victim of the sinking of the Lusitania, May 7th 1915.

WELSH WORDS

Pronunciations and meanings.

Ap – a contraction of the Welsh word 'mab' which means son. Dafydd ap Jones, translates as Dafydd, son of Jones.

Fy annwyl – pronounced: Fy – like making the phonic sound of an f; so, ff ann-well: translates as my dear

Bore da, Cariad – Pronounced as written: means – good morning, love

Cemaes Bay – Keh-mise Bay

Tŷ Glasfryn – Ne Glass-fer-ryn

Cwtch – cutch

Amlwch – Am-loo-ch (the ch make a guttural sound)

1

LLANEIRW, 1958

Silently, the old woman stood in the corner of the darkened room, unseen by the undertaker and his assistant. Most of the room was shrouded in a pallid light creeping through a gap between aged curtains, shrunk over time.

The body had already been prepared and carefully washed, her hair combed by a local nurse, paid for by the family. She'd also dressed the deceased in the clothes chosen by her relatives and, before leaving, had closed all the curtains in the house, in respect for the departed. Now, the undertaker, Dafydd ap Jones, was getting the body ready to be removed from the house.

Jones the Undertaker, as he was known locally, was smartly dressed and reverential in his task. With care, he'd arranged the dead woman's hands, folding them delicately across her waist. Then he'd made sure her silky, grey hair curled around the fine features of her face. Softly to the body, he whispered, "Rest in peace, *fy annwyl*," as though he was speaking to someone he knew. Dafydd liked to ensure he treated dead bodies as he would a living person – with the same dignity. He started to place a white sheet over the body but stopped midway.

"I always find it so sad when there is no family to say goodbye," he said to no one in particular. Certainly not to his assistant, who obviously didn't care one bit about the body they were preparing to take to the funeral home. He, Owen, was looking through the gap in the closed curtains at the seascape in front of him.

"Don't you find it sad?" Dafydd asked him.

"Find what sad, Mr Jones?" Owen looked annoyed about being interrupted.

"About this lady having no family nearby."

The old woman saw Owen give the body a derisory gaze before going back to his sea-watching. She'd been aware of his lack of care and mealy-mouthed manner as soon as he had come into her house.

Dafydd was used to his assistant's absence of interest and continued a conversation with himself. "At least she had relatives who sorted things out for her."

His mind went back to the conversation he'd recently had with Mrs Jane Armstrong, a very bossy but organised woman who'd told him exactly what was required in every single detail. He didn't mind people knowing what they wanted, especially when they paid promptly, which this lady had done. For example, she'd made it clear that her sister-in-law was to be buried wearing her engagement ring and wedding band. Daffyd had made a note to himself to keep an eye on that, as a few items of jewellery had gone missing recently.

Taking a quick glance over the body on the stretcher, he suddenly noticed that the covering sheet had a tiny hole in it. Almost invisible, yet he was mortified. He couldn't have the deceased leaving their home looking anything less than perfectly cared for.

"Owen," he said to his assistant, who was still staring out to sea, "I'm just going to get another sheet from the van." He knew he would just get mumbles and groans had he asked him to go.

"Okay, Mr Jones," Owen replied, without turning from the window. Something to his left along the beach had caught his eye, and his mind was totally engrossed with whatever it was.

However, as soon as Mr Jones had left the room, Owen walked over to the stretcher.

Earlier, he'd noticed a gold locket around the dead woman's neck. It looked expensive, and the perfect gift for his missus. Without ceremony or care, he removed it from the dead woman's neck. He quickly fluffed her hair back into place where it had moved, and as Mr Jones returned with the new sheet, he pocketed the locket. But he was in such a hurry that it missed his trouser pocket completely and fell onto the wooden floor, disappearing straight into a gap in the floorboards.

"What was that?" Mr Jones asked.

"Nothing," Owen replied, furious he'd not taken more care and had lost his ill-gained prize so easily.

He seemed to have got away with it. Jones the Undertaker replaced the sheet and indicated to Owen that it was time to move the body.

Together, the two men carefully negotiated the bend in the stairs and carried the body to the Jones & Son van. Dafydd hoped that one day soon, there would be a son.

For the first time since they'd arrived at her house, the woman, who had now moved to the bay window to watch the removal of her body, smiled.

She had waited for this moment for so long. For forty-three years, she'd yearned to see her love once more. She'd lived a solitary life filled with a few short memories of him, which sadly over the years had begun to fade. Yet, she still held him deep within her heart, although sometimes she found it hard to recall his face. She had the images that his family had given her, but it wasn't the same as holding him close, hearing his voice, hearing him humming a tune when he was happy. For those forty-three years, she'd pined for him. She'd hoped to be with him at last; she'd hoped they'd be reunited in death, for eternity.

But where was he? Her heart had already been broken once when he was taken from her all those years ago, but being unable to find him brought all those feelings back, and more. How could she ever rest when she couldn't find him? He wasn't in the afterlife, as she'd believed he would be.

She was grateful this mean, weaselly Owen was a thief. His greed meant a small part of her love was left in the house. Now she had hope of finding her beloved husband once more.

Watching, she saw Dafydd ap Jones come back and check they'd shut the front door securely. He closed the gate. She moved back into the shadows and settled to wait for help from the living.

Having waited four decades, she could wait a few more.

2

LLANEIRW, OCTOBER 2018

Jess looked around. The house seemed even drearier than she remembered it when her dad had dragged her there house-hunting. As selfish as she knew it was, Jess had wanted to stay where they were. Something was 'off' about this house. She couldn't put her finger on it, but it was the opposite of a welcoming atmosphere, and a musty smell constantly invaded all of her senses.

The removal van had left several hours ago; now it was just the two of them. She glanced over to where her dad was unpacking mugs. He looked up and smiled. Not one of the smiles he used to give, filling his entire face, but a smile that only just raised the corners of his mouth. Unable to watch his pretence at being happy, or remain in the dreary room any longer, Jess grabbed her hoodie, checked that her earbuds were in the pocket, and walked out, shouting "Bye" over her shoulder as she slammed the front door shut.

Standing in the gateway, Jess glanced back at the house, which looked so small compared to the one they had left. The tiny front garden was overgrown and dominated by a large bush, which hid the front door. When you drove into the driveway of their old house, you entered a magical world of trees that bent down to hug you. Wind chimes hung from the occasional branch, which rang out a welcome if a breeze caught them. As a youngster, she used to imagine families of fairies living in their haven. No fairies would grace this dismal space. The problem was, when they'd come to view the house, she wasn't in the mood to look, and she didn't care what they found. It wasn't going to be a real home. Nothing would ever be a home again, not without her mum.

Determined to dislike what she saw, Jess walked across the road to where a beach lay behind the seawall. Well, supposedly that's where the sea was, but who could tell through the grey haze enveloping everything? Today, only the sound of waves splashing against pebbles proved that the sea existed.

Why had her dad brought her here and to this particular house? What had he been thinking? The sea views might be okay in the summer, but even then, there was nothing amazing, and it wasn't even as though Llaneirw was lively. But she reasoned to herself that it didn't matter. Before long, she'd be gone, leaving for Manchester University.

To her right stood a church sheltered by trees that leant towards the building, as though sheltering it from the seaward winds. She couldn't face a church visit, so she crossed back to where their house was. They were one of thirteen detached and semi-detached 1930s houses, and Jess wondered who'd had the idea to build them here. Had it always been this quiet? Walking away from their gateway, she found a footpath at the end of the row that led under a bridge carrying the dual carriageway and railway track along the coast.

A café with the uncreative name 'The Walkers Rest' caught her attention. Glancing around, she wondered where on earth people would be walking to or from to 'rest'. Not in the mood for a walk into town, she ventured inside the café. She and her dad had got up incredibly early for the move, which now seemed hours ago, so she was beginning to feel peckish. Surprisingly, the café was quite busy, with several customers tucking into cakes and hot drinks. Her stomach rumbled as she smelled the food, so she went to look at the selection on offer.

The woman serving said, *"Bore da, cariad."*

Jess, still trying to make a choice of food, hadn't been fully listening when the woman spoke. Plus, she hadn't understood what was said as it didn't sound like English. The woman in front of her was a similar age to her mum, though this woman was what her mum would have called 'ample'.

Remembering her manners, Jess said, "Pardon?"

"Sorry. Good morning. What can I get you?"

Jess now couldn't decide whether to eat a snack or something more substantial, but feeling awkward, quickly decided. "A cappuccino and one of those chocolate cookies, please."

"I haven't seen you in here before. Are you staying in one of the cottages for a winter break?" the woman asked.

Jess didn't want to get into a big conversation, but she didn't want to appear rude. "No, not on holiday. We just moved into Number 17. Erm, me and my dad."

"Brilliant, it's about time we had some new blood moving into the village. I'm Anna. If you need anything, just knock. I live at Number 8, next door."

"Thank you, we're fine."

"You go and sit down, and I'll bring your drink and cookie over to you."

Jess chose a seat near the window and gazed out at the cul-de-sac around the café. Not much of a view with everything shrouded in mist. She assumed the six cottages slowly emerging from the mist must have been the holiday cottages Anna had spoken about. She looked around the café. Most of the other people appeared to be young mums plus a few older, probably retired people. It definitely wasn't the hub of excitement, but it was at least cosy and warm.

Anna appeared with her coffee and cookie, with the addition of a small, flat, round cake. "I hope you like it."

"I only ordered a cookie," Jess said, worried she had someone else's order.

"I always add a little Welsh cake for new customers. A little Welsh welcome. *Croeso*!" Anna disappeared behind the counter with a smile.

Jess decided to eat the Welsh cake first. It was like a mini pancake, but sweeter. At least she'd found one thing to brighten her day. The food was welcome, along with the hot coffee, plus talking to another human, rather than her dad, helped to lift her mood. She knew when she got home, they'd both return to their inarticulate limbo-land, making monosyllabic comments. It was as if they were strangers. The fact they didn't seem to know how to talk to each other saddened her. They'd always been so close and had a great relationship, but now – things were falling apart. She couldn't talk to him about how she was feeling, and she knew he was grieving too, but it was useless. What could she ever say to make him feel better, when she couldn't even help herself?

When she'd finished in the café, she walked back to the seawall and along the sea path to the left that led away from the cul-de-sac. She first passed the small gardens of the cottages, which then gave way to meadow land. After wandering some way, she came to a wooded area, where she decided to turn back.

On the return walk, she noticed a derelict building, which she guessed had been a farm, because there were several dilapidated outbuildings and barns. She assumed the cottages had once belonged to the farm, for their workers.

Back in the village, it appeared there was no one on holiday yet, so she peered in through one of the windows. She could see the house had been well renovated. The cottages looked cute, but she couldn't imagine who would want to come here for a holiday.

~

As soon as Jess had left, Danny stopped what he was doing and clung to the edges of the box as a wave of grief and anger swept through his body. 'Pull yourself together, man'. He let out a long, low sound, somewhere between a scream and a growl, and he threw one of the mugs he'd just unpacked at the wall. It smashed loudly, scattering pieces all over the floor.

Feeling annoyed with himself, he picked up the larger bits of pottery and threw them into a rubbish bag, leaving the rest to hoover up later. As he returned to his unpacking, he wondered where Jess had gone. He knew she wasn't happy with the move, though she was going to leave him on his own in a few months, so he had the right to choose where he was going to live. As soon as the thought left his mind, he felt guilty. He had gone through this inner conversation, over and over, before he'd even made the decision to move out of Liverpool. What he did know was, had he stayed, he'd have gone mad.

The front door banged shut behind Jess as she ambled back into the house. She had only been gone for a couple of hours, yet her dad looked as though he hadn't moved, and was still delving into boxes – although he'd managed to empty a few of those piled up in the living room and kitchen. At least he'd found the important utensils, like mugs and the kettle, and glasses so they could drink some of the many bottles of wine they'd been given as leaving presents.

"How was your walk?" Danny asked.

"Okay. I dropped into the little café for a coffee. Nice lady called Anna owns it. She offered her help if we ever needed anything."

"At least someone has made us feel welcome, then. So, what do you think?"

"It's just a bit quiet, but I suppose it'll do."

Danny looked up at her. "Don't complain. It's the seaside. I bet loads of people will want to come and visit us."

"What, to downtown Llaneirw? It's not quite the Costa del Sol, Dad. Can't see that happening, not when they can go to Spain or Greece." Seeing her dad's face drop, Jess added, "But at least it's not too far from Liverpool, so I suppose they might come over for a weekend."

Secretly, she was praying that some of her friends would come over. Soon. Her dad was still struggling with an answer. She hadn't meant to hurt him, but he was the one who'd made all the decisions about leaving. Packing up, moving them away from all their friends. She still couldn't understand why they just didn't move to somewhere else in Liverpool. Trying to lighten the mood, she asked, "Which boxes do you want me to unpack next?"

"Make a start in the bathroom, and then on your own room. Is it okay if we leave assembling your bed until tomorrow? You can sleep on the mattress for tonight, can't you? I'm going to do the same. I'm too tired after the move, and the unpacking."

In answer, Jess ran upstairs and dumped her hoodie onto one of the boxes piled up in her room, and then went into the bathroom. Putting her earbuds in, she turned on her latest playlist and hummed along while she went through the boxes to find the most important things they needed, like toothbrushes, loo rolls and shower gel. The avocado-green décor was just so hideous. Why anyone would choose it, she couldn't understand. It wasn't only that it was so dated, it was such a depressing colour. She was relieved that her dad had plans to make changes over the next few months. This was his project, and she knew that alongside his weird affection for the house, he needed the renovation to keep him occupied and busy.

It took no time at all to sort out the bathroom. Returning to her bedroom, she found the box that held her bedding and threw it onto the mattress. They'd brought some furniture from the old house, so at least she was able to hang some of her clothes. Next, she opened up the heaviest box that was full to the brim with books. Books for enjoyment, A-level course texts, and some she would be using when she started at Manchester. She arranged the books on her bookshelves in the corner of the room.

She had her desk too, which she'd placed under the bay window, to give her a sea view as she worked. Gradually, the desk began to take on her personality. There, she placed her laptop, a pile of notebooks with a cuddly mouse used for cleaning her laptop screen sitting on top, a tub of brightly coloured pens, useful office gadgets (including a staple remover she had never used but kept, just in case), and a couple of fun items like her squeezy stress hippo. The last thing to take its place on her desk was a photo of her with her parents, taken while on holiday in Italy a few years ago. Jess looked at it, reached out, and hugged it against her chest before carefully replacing it on the desk. It brought back memories of the day the photo was taken. A tear ran down her cheek. Her dad's voice jolted her back into the present, and she quickly wiped her face with the back of her hand.

"Do you fancy a pizza?" Danny shouted from downstairs.

Thinking it a bit early for dinner, Jess looked at her phone. To her surprise, it was already 7.00 p.m. "Please. Can I have pepperoni?"

Jess heard her dad ordering the pizzas and went downstairs to join him.

"How much did you get unpacked?" he asked.

"Enough for tonight. It'll be easier once the bed's put up. Have you finished all you wanted to do?"

"Yes, for now. I think I need a drink. Do you want something?"

Danny headed off to the kitchen to get himself a beer, with Jess following behind to see what was on offer. Most of the bottles of wine they'd been given were red, which Jess didn't drink, but there was a bottle of prosecco, so she opened that. Danny decided to forgo the beer and join her so they could toast the first night in their new home.

The pizzas arrived sooner than expected. Tucking into their food, neither of them wanted to talk, which put a dampener on any celebration. For much longer than was comfortable, they ate in complete silence. Eventually, Danny turned his iPod on so that music filled the void. Later, he mentioned that after they'd got the beds erected the next day, he was going to start thinking about the renovation.

"Where are you going to start?" Jess asked Danny, in between mouthfuls of pepperoni.

"I thought I'd make a start with the kitchen and this room. It would be nice to have somewhere presentable if we have any guests, or when people come around."

Jess looked at him as though he was speaking in some alien language, and far too quickly said, "Who are you expecting to visit? We don't know anyone here."

As soon as the words left her lips, it registered that, yet again, she was getting at him. She could tell by his face that the comment had hurt. "Sorry, Dad. I wasn't thinking."

He glanced up at her, giving her a weak smile.

Quickly, Jess continued. "I think it's a good idea to start down here. We need a decent kitchen." She took another bite of her pizza and then asked, "What are you planning."

"Are you sure you really want to know?"

"Yeah. Go on, Dad, tell me."

It was clear he'd been thinking about it in some detail, because he gave her a full explanation of how he was going to make the downstairs into an open-plan kitchen–living space, with a downstairs toilet and utility room.

It was the first time she'd heard her dad talk about anything with any energy at all. At last, he'd found something to turn his attention to. Something that would stop him from continually focusing on the accident. She hoped she could find something for herself too, because nothing seemed to lift her spirit for any length of time.

Jess refilled their glasses with more prosecco. "Here's to the new living space."

They smiled at each other, but it seemed both found it hard to keep the other's gaze. Neither wanted to see the emptiness reflected in their eyes. Jess was lost in her own world, and her dad was too. They slouched on the sofa. Danny's playlist wafted over them both and the surrounding array of unemptied boxes.

Sometime later, Danny stretched and said, "I'm going up to bed. All that unpacking has worn me out." He yawned.

"Okay, you poor old thing."

Danny took their glasses and the empty pizza boxes into the kitchen. Just as he was about to leave the room, he asked, "You got in touch with Manchester to tell them about our change of address, didn't you?"

"Yes! I did that as soon as we knew for definite we were moving here. They'll get in touch again when they need to. I've got most of the details I need anyway. They sent me term times a few months ago."

"Okay, I was just checking. We've had so much on our minds – wanted to make sure you hadn't forgotten them. The most important move for your future." He walked towards the stairs.

"You got everything you need to sleep okay tonight?" He came back and kissed Jess on the forehead.

"Yeah. See you in the morning. Night."

Jess decided she may as well go to bed too. Although she was tired, she wasn't ready to sleep yet. After switching off the living room lights, she checked that the front door was locked and went up to her room.

She changed into her pyjamas and plugged in her bedside lamp, grabbed the book she was reading, and settled down on the mattress. It wasn't half as uncomfortable as she'd expected. In fact, it was interesting sleeping at floor level. It gave a different perspective of the room.

A while after she'd started reading, her lamp began to flicker. "Oh, come on...don't die on me now." She switched on the torch on her mobile, then turned off the bedside lamp and checked that the plug was pushed fully into the socket. She switched the lamp back on. It seemed fine, so she turned her mobile torch off and returned to her reading.

A few minutes later, the flickering began again, and turning to look at it, she saw a blur of movement out of the corner of her eye. At the same time, a sudden chill in the room. She shivered. Shrugging her shoulders to get rid of the feeling, she turned her mobile torch back on, adding more light to the room. She shone the torch into each corner. Nothing was there. What did she expect to see? It was just the shadows created by the half-opened boxes against the walls.

She was far more tired than she'd thought. She closed her book and switched off her lamp, snuggling down into the warmth of her duvet, pulling it up tight around her neck. It reminded her of when she was a child and woke up, imagining there were monsters in her room. Lastly, she switched her mobile torch off, pushed it under her pillow, and closed her eyes tight.

In the darkest corner of the room, she silently watched the girl. All these years she'd waited for someone to notice her, even just be aware of a presence in the house. Yet not one single person had been open to the possibilities, and she had begun to lose all hope. Now, for the first time, she'd managed to make the bedside light visibly flicker. It must mean there was a connection. The girl had been aware of her presence. The girl had shivered and had pulled her bedclothes around her, so she was confident she was right. At last, here was someone with whom she could commune. Someone she would be able to reach out to across the divide.

She glided across the room to take a closer look at the girl who could possibly be spiritual enough to see her. Her long, dark hair lay tangled and strewn over her pillow. Her covers were pulled right up to her throat, as though their fluffy softness would protect her. The woman smiled, wishing she could snatch the bedclothes from her, shock the girl into waking, and then she would see her standing over the bed. She instantly chided herself for being so cruel. She had to be patient. It would take time to make the connection complete and be able to possess her.

The woman could feel the depth of grief filling the girl's soul. As soon as she and her father had entered the house, the enormity of their loss had spoken to her own enduring sorrow.

Unable to resist, she ran her hand over the girl's hair, and although she herself felt nothing, she saw the girl shudder in her sleep. "Soon," she whispered into the darkness. "Soon."

3

Waking from a heavy sleep, it took a while for Jess to realise where she was, and then she remembered she was in 'Llandreary-u', as she'd decided to rename it. She got up to look outside to see if it was as grey as yesterday. Amazingly, it looked much brighter, which made her feel a little more optimistic about things, so much so that she decided to make the effort to spend the day with her dad rather than disappear off on her own.

However, like most days, when she first woke, everything seemed fine until she remembered it wasn't. She would feel the hole deep inside her stomach, empty and aching as she remembered who was missing. It was the same each morning, but for the first time in months, there had been a glimmer that maybe things could get better.

After a quick shower, she pulled on her favourite joggers and jumper and went downstairs, where she could hear her dad banging around.

"How did you sleep, love?" he asked.

"Okay, once I'd got my lamp sorted out. It kept flickering. Don't know what was up with it. Did you sleep?"

"Yes, not bad." He yawned.

Jess wondered if he was lying. She suspected he hadn't actually slept through an entire night since the accident.

He swallowed another yawn and asked, "Do you want coffee?"

"Please." Jess poured herself a large bowl of granola.

"I'll check the sockets out for you later if you like?"

"Thanks, Dad."

After they'd eaten breakfast together, they spent the rest of the morning building both their beds and moving some of the heavier furniture into place. During the afternoon, they put all the unpacked boxes that they wouldn't need over the next few weeks into one of the spare rooms so that the main living spaces would look less cluttered. By early evening, the house was liveable. They could sit on the sofa without clambering over boxes and watch TV, now Danny had wired everything up.

This was the longest time they'd spent together in close proximity for ages, and even though today they hadn't had huge conversations, at least they'd been in the same room and had been civil with each other.

"Do you fancy going out for something to eat tonight, maybe try out the pub?" Danny asked, hoping that after the day they'd had, he could continue the positive interactions a little longer.

"Mm, do you think there'll be anyone there? I mean, it's not like we're in a metropolis," Jess said.

Danny was disappointed; he'd hoped she might at least want to find out what there was locally.

"It can't be that bad, surely. You never know, we might find it's a real gem," he said, trying to be enthusiastic.

"Have you noticed what it's called? 'The Blue Dolphin'. Not

very original, but suppose we've got to eat. Why not? Let's go and take a look."

Before Danny could say anything else, Jess had rushed upstairs to get her hoodie.

As they walked out of the house together, Danny said, "It's great that it's so close too. I want to have a beer or two after all our hard work unpacking these last two days. I know it's not the liveliest way to spend a Friday night, with your dad as a date, but..."

"It'll be fine, Dad. Come on, let's go and check out Llaneirw's nightlife."

They were soon tucking into plates of locally sourced seafood and chips, neither of them apparently realising just how hungry they were. Conversation was slow, but at least not non-existent, and an improvement on recent weeks. In between mouthfuls, Jess looked around the pub. She seemed pleasantly surprised and said it was far busier than she'd expected. There was a mixture of clientele, young and old. Probably locals, as it was several months away from the holiday season. Though, they must have driven here, or walked from town, because there weren't that many houses in this part of Llaneirw to even fill the bar, let alone the large restaurant that was in the modern extension.

Danny noticed a lad behind the bar, who had glanced over their way on several occasions.

"I think you've got a fan," he said to Jess, nodding towards the bar.

"Dad, don't be so embarrassing. I'm not sixteen." But she quickly glanced around to see who he was talking about, and then quickly turned back. She met the eyes of the guy with dark, curly hair. He was, in fact, staring at her.

"You realise I'm not coming here again!" she said.

Danny laughed.

They finished their meal and had a few more drinks. Danny left Jess alone at the table as he nipped to the loo.

Jess was busy scrolling through her phone when she was aware of someone hovering next to her. The guy from the bar.

"Are you okay if I clear these? Have you finished?" he asked, smiling down at her.

She nodded.

"You on holiday? I've not seen you in here before."

"We've just moved here." She saw him raise an eyebrow. "Me and my dad," she added quickly, then felt stupid for qualifying who she was with.

"O-kaaaay," he answered, adding a slight laugh, and again, the raised eyebrow. "Hope to see you here again soon then." Smiling again, he walked away with the empty plates and glasses just as Danny reappeared.

"C'mon, let's go," said Jess, pulling him out of the pub.

"Did I miss something?" he asked.

"Nothing!" she replied, starting to walk quickly across the car park to their cul-de-sac.

On the very short walk home, which Jess' gran would have called a 'hop, skip and jump', Danny mentioned that the next day, he was going to make a start on the kitchen renovation. He asked her if she wanted to help him. Jess didn't know that she'd be any use, but said she was happy to try, especially if it meant pulling things down. She quite fancied the idea of being able to demolish a wall.

Settling down to watch TV, Danny stretched out on the sofa. Jess said goodnight and told him she was going up to her room to read for a while before sleeping.

Once she'd got herself comfortable on her newly built bed, she started reading but after a while put her book aside. Something she had read reminded her of her school friends. After her mum's accident, several people she considered to be friends had made excuses not to invite her to events and only ever chatted for a short time. She understood things were awkward, but she'd hoped they would have made a better effort. At least her three best friends had supported her. Jess scrolled through their profiles on her phone to see what they were up to.

Most were in their first terms at university. She scrolled past pictures of her friend Anika, out at a club with new friends in Bristol, then Jamie, pictured in his new hall of residence, and lastly her best friend, Sammie, with a group of girls she looked close to already, in a bar, drinking cocktails. A tear ran down her face, and she angrily wiped it away. No one else was to blame. It had been her choice to defer going to Manchester University this year. She'd discussed it with her dad and the university; they'd been very supportive, ultimately advising her that because she was a 'summer baby' who'd had a recent trauma, it would be sensible for her to wait a year and begin next September. Without the energy to give it much thought, she'd agreed. Now she was beginning to wonder if she'd done the right thing.

Annoyed with both herself and her friends, none of whom had even texted to ask how the move had gone, she threw her phone on the floor. Still fully clothed, she crawled under her duvet. At least tonight she was sleeping in her actual bed, rather than just on the mattress, so she should get a good night's sleep, and she might even dream about the guy in the pub.

The water was cold and deathly black. Try as hard as she might, she was battling to hold her breath and was terrified, wondering whether she'd be able to maintain it any longer. Thrashing her arms and legs, she strove to push herself towards the surface, where she could see daylight, but something was holding her down. The problem was her heavy, cumbersome clothes. Her lungs felt as though they would explode at any minute. Again, she pushed with all her might, but she couldn't help swallowing mouthfuls of the salty brine. Her whole body ached, and she began to think she should just let go. She seemed to have been fighting against the water for ages. *Please, let the water take me and put me out of my misery,* she thought, as if in prayer. But somewhere in the distance, far, far above her, she could hear muffled voices. Suddenly hands grabbed her hair, which had come loose from its clips and was floating in the water, then strong arms reached out and pulled her from the water to safety.

Jess tried to wake, gasping for air, the smell of seawater engulfing her senses. Trying to take a deep breath was incredibly hard. A sound echoed around her bedroom, and it was a while before she registered that it was her. Screaming.

Danny rushed in and turned on the light. He grabbed his daughter up into his arms.

"Jess, love. Whatever's the matter?" He pulled her closer. "You're soaking wet!"

She gasped for air.

"Breathe. Come on, love, breathe. What on earth's been going on?" Danny asked.

Eventually, Jess' breath became more even, and gradually, she calmed down.

"What happened, love?"

"Oh, God, Dad, I don't know. I was dreaming. I...I was drowning, but it wasn't me. It was weird. I could see her, but at the same time, I felt everything she was going through. It was like I was in two places at once."

Danny kissed her forehead. "But how did you get wet? I don't understand."

Still violently shaking, Jess put her hands on her body. "Shit, I don't know, Dad. I don't know what happened. It was like a dream, but I heard everything and felt the sensations, as though I was in her body."

"Let's get you dry, and you can come and sleep in my room. Okay?"

Jess nodded, and Danny stepped outside the door while she got changed.

Once she was in her warm PJs, Danny guided her up to his room, the largest in the house, and the one that needed the most work doing to it. As well as his bed, there was a sofa. He got Jess tucked up into his bed and remained hugging her until she eventually fell asleep.

Danny sat on the edge of the bed, looking down at his daughter. She had been through so much this year. Maybe he'd been in too much of a rush to move away from Liverpool. He'd been thinking about himself; perhaps he hadn't considered Jess' feelings enough. But things had been going so well today, until this bad dream.

This was unusual for her. She hadn't even had nightmares as a young girl. He and Kate had always commented on how well-adjusted Jess was. He'd only just appreciated that he'd taken this for granted over the last few months. He made a vow to himself to be more thoughtful in the future.

He was glad she was sleeping soundly now. The sofa didn't look quite as inviting as his bed, but he slept poorly these days anyway, so he knew it wouldn't make much difference.

When Danny woke, Jess was already up, and as if nothing had happened, he found her sitting on the edge of her bed looking around the room.

"I've been thinking, I want to change the colours in here and brighten it up. Can I buy some paint and make a start?" she asked.

Danny was surprised. That hadn't been the conversation he'd expected.

"Yes, we can go and get some this morning if you like?" he answered, pleased that she seemed brighter. "Have you got over last night's dramatic dreams?" he asked tentatively.

"Yes, I'm feeling much better. I don't know where that dream came from. Maybe it was because I went to sleep with all of my clothes on and was too hot. Perhaps it's the smell of the sea and being able to hear it at night. I don't know, but I'm fine today. Sorry I woke you."

Later, Jess waited, holding the back gates open while her dad got the car out of the garage to go and buy the decorating stuff for her bedroom. Unused to having a garage at the bottom of the garden, Jess found it odd. Looking around, it was obvious how much work the garden would need when the house was finished. She smiled to herself, hoping she might have left by then. Gardening wasn't her thing.

A terrible scraping sound alerted Jess to someone opening gates at the house next door, Number 16.

"Hello," a female voice sang out, the way some older women's voices do.

Jess looked around to see who was talking. Peering out of

their entrance, she saw a very short woman in her late fifties, standing next to a red Mini.

The woman continued. "How's the move going?"

"Fine, thanks."

"Good. I'm Alison and my husband is Paul. If you need anything, just give us a knock. We're always happy to help."

"Thanks. I'm Jess and—" Just at that point, her dad appeared, having battled to shut the garage doors. "And this is my dad, Danny."

"Pleased to meet you both. Don't forget, we're here to help."

With a little wave, she got in her car and drove off.

"Well, now we know the natives are friendly," Danny commented.

Danny and Jess had returned from the DIY store where they'd bought all the things needed to paint Jess' room. Jess had disappeared to make a start. She'd gone up to cover her bed and furniture with sheeting, and lay out the brushes, rollers, and the interesting range of colours she'd chosen. Danny was intrigued to see what the finished room would look like when he'd seen the mixture of teals and gold paints, but he kept any doubts to himself. He had told Jess not to worry about getting paint on the floor; he would take the carpet up and sand the floorboards.

Jess didn't even come down for any lunch, though Danny took up a cup of coffee and sandwiches. She made him leave them outside her room. "Don't come in. You can't see it until it's finished," she yelled as he was about to open the door.

The house was a hive of activity. Danny started to remove the tiles from the kitchen splashbacks and take down some of the cupboards while Jess was busy upstairs. Both of them locked in their individual worlds.

For a break from dismantling the kitchen, Danny had nipped out while Jess was painting and had got some food to cook. He yelled up to her that dinner was ready if she was. She rushed down, apparently without considering what she looked like. Danny laughed when he saw her. Her hair was streaked with gold paint, and her arms and hands were also splattered with gold and teal.

"You look like an art installation," he said, smiling. "Wash your hands and we can eat. You can shower later."

A heavy weight lifted from Danny's chest. Today was the first time he had laughed. A laugh that had come from within himself, allowing a small amount of grief to escape from the depths where it had been firmly squatting. As Jess walked past him to the sink, he grabbed her and kissed her hair.

"Am I allowed to see the work of art, or do you want me to wait until tomorrow, in the daylight?" he asked.

"I think, wait until later tomorrow. I should have finished it by then. I managed to get a lot done today, working with rollers, but there's a little more to finish." Then as an afterthought. "Can I sleep in your room again tonight too? I don't fancy the smell of paint that much."

"Of course, you can." Danny was pleased she'd asked, though wondered if the paint was an excuse. He didn't want to count his chickens too soon, but it seemed they were getting their relationship back on track.

As good as her word, by the end of the next day, Jess called Danny up to her room to see what she'd done. He was pleasantly surprised. The wall behind her bed was painted in a rich gold, and then other walls in teal, with the ceiling painted a slightly lighter-coloured teal. It looked amazing, although he quickly recognised that there would be extra spending required for new bedding and curtains or blinds. If Jess was anything like Kate, things had to match!

Together they decided to leave the extras until the floor had been done, which would also have to wait, because while Jess was painting, Danny had removed much of the existing kitchen. He was, however, waiting to let her help him demolish the main wall between the kitchen and lounge. He knew she was looking forward to that. Besides, he wasn't quite ready to be completely without a kitchen straight away after the move. They had enough going on as it was. Plus, he needed to contact the plumber to make a date so they could move the piping around to fit the new kitchen he'd ordered. True to his wife's word, Paul next door had been helpful and had given Danny the number of a reputable plumber, which he was grateful for, not knowing any local tradesmen.

~

The very first night Jess was back in her room, she woke again, soaking wet, and gasping for breath. This time the dream started earlier in the event. Jess jumped from the side of a large ship into a lifeboat. But as it was being lowered to the sea below, one of the ropes snapped, and as it hit the water, the boat overturned, spilling everyone over the side into the murky depths. People around her were screaming, and other bodies bumped into her as she fell. The shock of the cold made her gasp, as she sank into the water's blackness. As in her previous dream, she was madly trying to push herself to the surface, but this time, Jess understood why her clothes had been so heavy and had held her under the water. She had noticed what she was wearing while standing on deck. An ankle-length tweed skirt, a high-necked blouse and low heeled, lace-up shoes and, of course, a life jacket. Before jumping into the sea, her long, mouse-coloured hair was neatly done in an 'up do', but as she had fought and failed to keep afloat in the water, her hair had become loose, which had in fact been her saving grace. When Jess woke from this dream, yet again she was soaking wet.

Despite her newly painted room, all she could smell was seawater. Luckily, this time, she hadn't woken her dad. She shakily scrambled out of bed, dried herself off and, yet again, put on a dry pair of PJs. Keeping the light on, she crawled back into bed and sat up, too scared to fall asleep and dream again.

She could picture the woman clearly, but who was she, and why was she dreaming about her? It wasn't anyone she knew, and she herself had never experienced drowning and hadn't seen anyone else drown either. So where had this all come from?

She tried hard to keep her eyes open, but in the end, still sitting up, she fell asleep.

Jess woke around 8.00 a.m. when the morning light was beginning to creep in through her old curtains. Not fully awake, she glanced over towards the bay window and blinked several times to clear her eyes, thinking she was seeing things. An older woman stood in the bay window, gazing out to sea. Jess became aware that there was no sound from either inside or outside the room. She could no longer hear the waves washing over the pebble beach, or the clock on the landing that normally irritated her. Very slowly, the woman turned towards Jess.

The woman had white hair and a gentle smile. She whispered to Jess. *Don't be scared. It's my story. I want you to see my story.*

Though the woman hadn't actually whispered her words audibly, somehow the words were inside Jess' head. Then as suddenly as she had appeared, the apparition, which is the only way Jess could describe her, was gone.

The sounds of the day returned, along with Jess' heart beating so loudly it echoed around her head. She leapt out of bed and ran out of the door and up to her dad's room.

"Dad, Dad." She shook him from out of his sleep. "There was a woman in my room."

Half awake, Danny rushed out of bed and followed Jess down to her room. "There's no one here, love. You must have been dreaming."

"But there was, Dad, honestly. I think it was the woman I've been dreaming about – she told me not to be scared and that she was sharing her story with me."

"Jess, love, I think you must have still been dreaming. I'll bring you a warm drink up. Why don't you go back to sleep for a while?" He disappeared downstairs.

Jess knew he meant well, but he didn't believe her. She knew she hadn't imagined it; she wasn't some hysterical child. It dawned on her that the old woman must be the younger one she'd dreamt about. Maybe she would see more in the next dream – if she had another? Not that she really wanted another dream, because experiencing the feeling of drowning was horrendous. But, the woman was obviously trying to connect with her.

Over the next few days, Jess continued to dream and, each time, with every nightmare, a little more of the story unfolded. In one dream she saw the ship's huge funnels sinking towards where people were thrashing about in the water. As the disaster unfolded, it became more terrifying each time.

She also caught sight of the older woman several times, but only ever in her room. Never anywhere else in the house, and her dad never saw her at all.

The latest dream had begun at the point where the ship

started to list, and very quickly, one side of the ship was high above them. The woman was desperately calling out someone's name. Panicking, she scrambled along the sloping deck, trying to remain on her feet, weirdly, away from the lifeboats. All the time, she cried out the name of the person she couldn't find. Other passengers who knew her were begging her to get to safety. In the end, they had to hold her and pull her towards the boats waiting to be lowered into the sea.

On that occasion, when Jess woke, not only was she soaked to the skin, but she was sobbing uncontrollably, the feeling of loss overpowering her entire being. This was the worst dream she'd suffered. She understood the feeling of grief only too well.

When Jess finally came downstairs for breakfast, Danny was shocked by her appearance. "Jess, love..." He knew he had to do something. "Maybe you should go to the doctors and see if you can get some sleeping pills? We need to sign up with them anyway."

"Seriously? Dad, this woman is trying to tell me something, I'm sure of it. I just don't know what."

"How do you know she's real? These could just be a series of bad dreams," Danny said.

"I've never had bad dreams before, even after Mum..." Jess stopped mid-sentence. "Even then I didn't have bad dreams. I'd have thought you might have done, but I haven't." She continued. "I keep seeing her too! It didn't happen just the once. She is often in my room looking out to sea."

Danny looked at his daughter as though she was mad.

Of course, he'd dreamt about Kate. Whenever he shut his eyes to sleep, he could picture her car, over and over again. Which was exactly why he couldn't sleep, because he couldn't not see that terrible, haunting image. He didn't believe in ghosts.

He didn't want to believe in ghosts. If he did, then surely, he would be able to see Kate? Even living back in the old house, where she had died, he hadn't seen her. He couldn't accept that Jess was getting messages from some apparition. It wasn't fair when he couldn't see the woman he loved, yet Jess could see this woman – a stranger.

"I'm sorry you don't believe me, Dad." Jess took her bowl of granola and stomped back up to her room.

Surrounded by smashed tiles that had broken as he'd removed them, and some of the dismantled cupboards, Danny remained sitting in what was beginning to look like a disaster site. It matched his mood. He was beginning to think he'd been selfish to have made the move before Jess had gone to university. Keeping busy to try to keep their mind off their feelings had failed miserably. They'd been at the house for over a week now, and nothing seemed to be going smoothly.

That night, as Jess dreamed, the woman watched over her, standing at the foot of her bed. This girl had felt her own loss too. Although the woman hated seeing the girl filled with the fear and terror she had experienced as the boat sank, she needed her to understand what had happened. Above all, she needed her to feel the utter despair of losing her soulmate and the love of her life. They would help each other deal with their losses. She was sure of it.

4
LIVERPOOL, FEBRUARY 2018

As Danny neared home, the traffic was backed up, which was unusual for roads in the quiet Liverpool suburb where they lived. He turned into Fernley Road and could see, where their house was, the road was blocked with two fire engines, an ambulance and police cars. He panicked when he recognised the little red car that was concertinaed almost into a box, squashed far too close to the skip outside a neighbour's house.

It was Kate's car.

Danny threw his bicycle down and raced towards the emergency vehicles, screaming out her name. A policeman tried to stop him from getting any closer to the wreck, but Danny was frantic to know that it wasn't Kate, and he pushed the policeman so hard he almost knocked him over. He barged past, running towards the mangled mess of metal that had once been a car. He almost reached the car before being stopped by several pairs of sturdy hands that held him tightly while he struggled to get free.

"Don't, Danny. You don't want to go any closer. You can't do anything."

A voice he knew, but couldn't quite place.

He turned to find out who was speaking. It was Geoff, his friend and next-door neighbour. He was as white as a sheet. The other hands belonged to a fireman and another policeman.

"Geoff – what happened? Please, tell me that isn't Kate's car? It can't be. Why would it be smashed so close to home?"

He knew in his heart it was her car. But he couldn't fathom how on earth Kate's car could be so badly damaged, when she couldn't have been driving very fast.

"I'm so sorry, mate, she's gone," Geoff said quietly.

All at once, Danny lost the use of his legs and his whole body began to shake. The next minute, Geoff and a paramedic were leading him towards the ambulance. On the way, he suddenly threw up. "I'm sorry..."

"Don't worry, it's the shock," the paramedic said as he put a blanket around Danny, who was still shaking as they led him into the back of the ambulance and onto a seat.

Turning to Geoff, the paramedic said, "You can leave him with me. Is there anyone else from the family who will be coming home soon?"

"Oh, God, yes. Their daughter, Jess. I'm surprised she isn't home yet."

The paramedic turned to Danny. "Do you know when Jess is coming home? We don't want her to see all of this."

Clarity returned to him as soon as the paramedic mentioned Jess' name. "She's not coming home tonight. She's staying with a friend. I need to tell her...How am I going to tell her?"

Danny looked up at Geoff and the paramedic, imploring them to give an answer that no one could give. He sank back into the seat, clinging to the blanket that had been placed around his shaking body. Tears began to fall down his face as he sobbed uncontrollably.

Danny remembered very little of the rest of the day. People came and went, yet he remained in a daze. Geoff and his wife, Jackie, made sure he wasn't on his own. Danny wanted to stay in his own house, so one of them remained with him in case he needed anything.

Having to break the news to Jess was the second worst moment of his life. Initially, she'd gone quiet and then started screaming. Even when Danny held her tight against his chest, she continued to emit a strange unworldly wail.

The police had removed Kate's car the evening of the accident, after extracting her mangled body from the wreckage. The only physical evidence of there ever being an accident was skid marks on the road's tarmac. Danny was glad that, at least, Jess hadn't had to witness the physical carnage of the tragedy.

A few days later, when the police had finished their investigations into the accident, Geoff sat alongside Danny in the front room where, only a few days earlier, Kate had sat snuggled up next to him, watching TV. The young policeman who had introduced himself, whose name Danny had already forgotten, explained how the accident had happened.

"A police vehicle had been in pursuit of a young lad who had stolen a high-performance car. He had driven down Fernley Road far too fast, lost control, and was on the wrong side of the road. A lorry full of building supplies was coming in the opposite direction and had swerved to miss the oncoming car. He swerved to his right, rather than left, because there were pedestrians on the pavement on his side of the road, but he hadn't seen your wife, who was coming out of your drive, on the right-hand side of Fernley Road. He smashed into the side of her car, pushing her into the skip. The collision between the heavy lorry and your wife's car caused the Smart car's chassis to completely buckle."

The young policeman took a breath and quickly glanced up at Danny. He took a quick sip of the tea Geoff had made for him, before continuing. “The young lad escaped the scene, but was caught later, and will be charged with dangerous driving, among other things.”

Geoff put his hand on Danny’s shoulder.

Danny managed to form a question. “What happened to the lorry driver?”

“He went to hospital, suffering from severe shock, and also some minor lacerations and injuries,” the policeman replied, then added, “He will be interviewed later.”

Danny took a loud intake of breath. “How...what...?”

He didn’t seem able to get out the words he wanted. Geoff was obviously thinking the same and asked, “Why is he being questioned when it was the young lad who caused the entire accident?”

The policeman took a while to answer. “That’s the law, sadly. Even though the lad caused the accident, it was the lorry driver who hit your wife’s car.”

Danny managed to compose himself and said, “Surely, though, ‘the Law’ will be more lenient with the lorry driver? It sounds as though he just reacted, thinking he would avert an accident. It must have happened so quickly for the poor man.”

“The case will be looked at by the CPS, including the evidence of the two pursuit police drivers, and they will make a decision about charges. I’m sure if the matter goes to court, they will consider any mitigating circumstances.”

“So, what will the joyrider be charged with?” Danny asked, thinking how inappropriate the word ‘joy’ seemed in this situation.

“There are several charges. Unlawful taking of a car, not holding a driving licence or having insurance, and causing death by dangerous driving.”

In the days following the accident, Danny had had to identify Kate's body, despite her being so badly disfigured that there weren't many features he could identify. Much of her body was covered, yet it had still been far more traumatic than he could ever have imagined. He was given her engagement and wedding rings, plus her bag, shoes and the other jewellery she'd been wearing, which had incredibly managed to escape the accident relatively unscathed.

Walking back to Geoff's car, Danny clutched the bag containing Kate's belongings, trying to rationalise what he'd just seen. He was grateful that Geoff had offered to drive him to the morgue. He certainly couldn't have driven himself home after visiting – and imagining what he hadn't been allowed to see. He was glad Jess had made the decision not to see her mum. He wanted her to remember her as she had been: alive and vivacious.

During the time leading up to the funeral, Danny and Jess lived in a strangely quiet, frozen world where nothing made any sense to either of them. Since Danny had told her the news, Jess had spent most of the time in her own room. Danny had checked on her periodically, knowing there was little he could do to help her, because he couldn't even help himself. He couldn't sit anywhere for long. When he sat on the sofa, he missed the feeling of Kate's feet pushing into his legs, or resting on his lap; her comments when they watched films, telling him what was coming, and how she always cried so easily, even at cartoons. There was no calm place where he could sit and remember happier times. Instead, a constant ache lingered. She'd been horrifically snatched from him, and he'd been unable to say goodbye. He and Jess ate in silence and walked around each other in the house, treating each other as though they were made of porcelain. Neither seemed to be able to name the awful thing that had happened to them, fearing they would crumble into grieving wrecks.

By the time the case came to court, almost two months after the accident, Danny had already decided he couldn't remain living in the house on Fernley Road. It held too many memories, and each time he drove or cycled out of the driveway, his whole body felt the horror of the night he'd ridden home and seen the accident. Now he knew what PTSD felt like. He had been seeing a therapist for some time, which was helping, but he knew in his heart there was no way he could live there any longer. But it wasn't just that. The court's decision forced his hand.

The CPS had decided that there would be no proceedings against Jim James, the lorry driver, as he wasn't responsible for the death. As a witness, standing in court, Jim looked a broken, desperate man.

After the hearing, Jim walked up to Danny. He broke down, unable to look Danny in the face. Danny put his hand on Jim's shoulder to console him, telling him how he knew it wasn't his fault.

Young Sean Brody, though, had no problem standing up in court. He gazed around, looking cocky and confident, without the slightest evidence of any remorse whatsoever. It took all of his control for Danny to remain quiet and seated next to Geoff on one side, and Jess on the other, who had wanted to come and hear the verdict. Sean Brody, just as the policeman had said, was charged with the unlawful taking of a car, not holding a driving licence or having insurance, and causing death by dangerous driving. To Danny's horror, he was only given five years, but would probably be out after two. Five years for causing the death of his beloved Kate, his soulmate. A wonderful mother and an amazing teacher. How could this kid be allowed to get away with it! Five years in prison would probably be a breeze for him. He'd probably meet up with other mates, already inside. Danny was seething because it was completely out of his control.

That was the point when he made the decision to move out of Liverpool. If they stayed, he couldn't face the fact that, some day in the future, Sean Brody would be walking around the city, and they could even walk down the same street. Yes, it meant an upheaval for him and Jess, but she was leaving for university, anyway. He spent a lot of time debating the situation. If he remained, he'd be alone in a place that reminded him of the accident, every single day. His heart would be broken, living without Kate.

The very next day, he put the house on the market, and after he'd looked at properties online, he and Jess had driven to Llaneirw to look at a house on the seafront, in need of some renovation and modernisation. He wasn't thinking of a forever home, but a project to keep him busy. It was certainly very different to where they lived now – a buzzing suburb of a major city. Llaneirw was a coastal village. The North Wales Expressway bypassed the village and left it alone to quietly sleep while drivers sped past on a faster route around the coast. Danny wanted a change, and there was nothing to stop him moving again, once he'd renovated the property. He didn't want time to think; he wanted something to take his mind off his loss.

Danny ran his own business, which was doing well, and he knew that his staff could easily run it without him. He would still be the CEO, but he could hand it over to them to run the day-to-day organisation and production. In fact, he'd already been planning to step away, having built up a strong enough team to cope without him. Once Jess had gone to university, he and Kate had been planning to do more travelling. Sadly, that would no longer be the case, but at least he didn't have to worry about the business.

When he told Geoff and Jackie, they said they were sorry he was going to leave, but they understood why he'd made the decision. Jess wasn't too happy about it, though. Danny reasoned that most of her friends were going to university too, so she would most likely lose touch with some of them, whether she was in Liverpool, Wales, or Manchester. In Danny's experience, most people who went away to university rarely came back to live in the same town. Well, at least, that's what had happened during his time. But when you have good friends, you can keep in touch wherever you are. And, of course, she'd make new friends at university.

The sale of the house in Fernley Road went through very quickly. It was a detached property, built in the 80s, but had been renovated in the last two years. Danny got more than the asking price, and four months after the sale was agreed, he and Jess moved to Llaneirw to start what he hoped would be their new life.

5
LLANEIRW, 2018

Danny worked on less noisy jobs while Jess was asleep. She'd seemed to be sleeping longer recently, which he was sure was because of her bad dreams. He couldn't believe she was seeing ghosts. He didn't want to believe that. Besides, he hadn't seen a thing, so he put it down to her continuing grief, plus the upheaval of the move. That had all been his idea, because he couldn't face living where Kate had died. But he was beginning to understand that his grief wasn't like Jess'. More and more, he was realising how insensitive he'd been.

Danny had promised Jess that she could help him knock down the wall between the kitchen and lounge. He decided today was the day, and he hoped that the physical exertion of some heavy hitting might help her get rid of some of her pent-up emotion. He stopped what he was doing as he at last heard some movement from upstairs.

On his way up the stairs with a coffee for her, Danny met Jess halfway.

"Morning! How did you sleep?" A redundant question, because her dishevelled look told him everything he needed to know.

“I don’t know why you waste your time asking me, because you don’t believe me when I tell you about my dreams.”

Her reply matched her demeanour.

Ignoring her comments, he asked, “Do you still want to help knock the kitchen wall down today? I’ve been saving it for you to help.”

Without any comment, Jess walked past him, taking the cup of coffee from him as she went. After searching for and finding the cereal, she helped herself then sat down on the sofa, which was about the only seat not covered with rubbish. “Once I’ve eaten my breakfast, I’ll get changed.”

Danny returned to the kitchen to prepare the space around the wall that was to be demolished. The only remaining evidence that it had been a kitchen was the sink and the cooker. Everything else had been removed, and the food and dishes were stacked in the lounge at the far end, covered in a large sheet of plastic. It was a messy business, trying to renovate when you lived in the property. He’d done it before, but on that occasion, he’d been more organised, plus Kate had helped too. On his own, he hadn’t fully considered the disruption it would cause. He had at least moved some things into the garage and had stacked other stuff they needed to be able to access easily in the spare room. He’d become too comfortable living in the larger space of their previous home.

An hour later, both of them were in the kitchen, where Jess was helping to bash hell out of half the adjoining wall to the lounge. There wasn’t time for conversation. She put all of her energy into each swing of the mini-sledgehammer as she pummelled the wall with great enthusiasm. They took it in turns and by lunchtime the wall was down. They cleared up the rubble and put it into the new skip, which had replaced the overly full one that had been previously parked in front of their house.

"I think we deserve a coffee and some of that cake we bought the other day, don't you?" Danny asked, speaking for almost the first time since they'd started the work.

Jess nodded. While her dad was boiling the kettle in the lounge area, she sat cross-legged on one of the old kitchen chairs, at last looking more relaxed than he'd seen her in days.

"You'll sleep well tonight!" Then catching her look, he wanted to bite his own tongue. "I mean it. You might get a good sleep after all that hard work."

"I doubt it," Jess replied.

He wanted to broach the subject of her dreams but was scared to ruin the moment. The demolition work seemed to have relaxed her, but he knew he could easily destroy the atmosphere by saying the wrong thing. Oh, the joy of having teenagers.

Jess saved him the trouble by starting a conversation herself. "Dad, I'm not making up my dreams or that I'm seeing this woman. It's real. She's real – well, I can see her."

Danny took time to consider his reply. He had the feeling that whatever he said would be wrong. "I'm sorry, but I find it hard to understand. I don't believe in ghosts, so I find it hard that you're really seeing someone and that it isn't purely a continuation of your dream. There has to be a logical explanation."

"Seriously, Dad. You think I'd be feeling so disturbed if they were normal dreams?"

Jess instantly lost any composure she'd gained over the last few hours. "Do you think I'm stupid because I'm seeing a ghost?"

"No, of course not, love. I think it's part of your grief affecting your sleep." Danny moved towards her to hug her, but she shrugged him away.

"But you do think that. You're not listening to me, and you don't believe me. I know what I'm seeing, and it's more than just nightmares. It's...It's something else completely." Tears began to creep down her cheeks, which she hastily wiped on her sleeve.

"Jess, love. I want to help, but I don't know how."

"Maybe you should talk to Mum's 'woo-woo' friend, as you used to call her. She'd tell you that you're wrong. That ghosts do exist."

Jess stormed out and rushed up to her room.

Danny ran his hands through his hair in frustration. He didn't know what to do. Normally, he could ask Kate. In fact, in the past, the three of them had been a close-knit unit, and together they'd been able to talk things out, no matter how difficult or upsetting. However, Kate had been the fulcrum who had kept everyone and everything around her calm. In this moment, Danny felt her loss more deeply than he had done since the actual day of her death. Now his cheek was damp with tears. *Kate, how am I going to cope without you?* He let the tears fall, allowing his grief to engulf him.

Upstairs, clothes were strewn all over Jess' bedroom floor, as she'd stripped off the dust-covered jeans and T-shirt. After showering, she lay on her bed, looking up at the ceiling she'd recently painted. She was thinking about her 'visitor'. She certainly wasn't any figment of imagination from her dreams. The woman had appeared to her regularly. Mostly, she was standing in the bay window, next to Jess' desk, looking out to sea. Sometimes, though, when Jess woke from her drowning dreams, the woman was standing at the bottom of her bed. On these occasions, oddly, her presence didn't particularly scare Jess. It was as though she was watching over her, like her mum had done when she was little and had woken in the night. Jess certainly wasn't being stupid or over-dramatic, and definitely not 'woo-woo'. She'd had enough of being cooped up inside. She needed to escape for a walk by the sea, and grabbing her warm hoodie, ran downstairs. She yelled "Bye" to her dad, as she ran out, not even waiting to hear his reply.

When Danny had said "Bye" to Jess, his voice had been hoarse from trying, yet failing, to contain his emotion. Danny found the box containing the strong liquor. He pulled out the bottle of Macallan single malt whisky, and after pouring himself a large glass, settled down on the sofa. Taking a swig, he savoured the mild burn as the liquor reached his throat, followed by the lingering sweetness that always reminded him of caramel. He shut his eyes and recalled the time he and Kate visited the distillery in Craigellachie, on the banks of the River Spey, while on a touring holiday in Scotland. She'd never been a fan of Scotch but loved the taste of Macallan, which is why they'd always had a bottle in the house ever since. The warmth of the liquid began to melt his mood. He thought about Sally, Kate's friend. When he'd finished his drink, he would ring her and see if she could make any suggestions, although she'd be very surprised that he had rung her. He was a little nervous of her, if truth be told. She didn't suffer fools, and he always got the impression she'd decided that was exactly what he was.

Danny dialled Sally's number, fortified with his 'Dutch courage'.

"Hi, Sally." He paused. He hadn't considered getting an answerphone. "Erm, I wanted to chat to you about something that I think you may be able to help me with." He paused again. That sounded far too vague, so he continued. "Jess has been having bad dreams and she thinks she's seeing someone. Can you give me a buzz when you pick this message up, please? Thanks." As he was about to cut the message off, he remembered he hadn't said who he was, so quickly added, "It's Danny, by the way."

Part of him was relieved she was out, but then that was a bit of a cowardly reaction. He hoped Sally would ring while Jess was still out.

~

After leaving the house, Jess strode down the road, walking as fast as she could. With her anger dictating her stride, she marched under the bridge and quite a way into the main part of Llaneirw, barely noticing anything around her. Eventually, she calmed down enough to head back.

On the way, Jess dropped into Anna's Café again. This time the lady greeted her like a long-lost friend, which, although nice, was a bit weird too. Jess took a large mug of hot chocolate and two Welsh cakes over to a seat by the window. After a while, she noticed another girl around her age sitting a few tables away. She was busy typing on a laptop, and looking up, she smiled. Jess returned the smile.

A scruffy backpacker walked in and dumped his bag by a table in the corner to mark it as his. He ordered a coffee and a sandwich, which he was served, plus his 'first-time visitor' Welsh cake. "I didn't order this," he said, very loudly and abruptly to Anna. As she'd done on Jess' first visit, she explained about the Welsh welcome. "Well, I don't want it, so you can keep it, thank you."

He grabbed his drink and sandwich and sat down in a corner, away from everyone else. Although no one spoke, the shocked reaction to his rudeness from everyone in the café was palpable. He must have been very thick skinned, because several people continued to glare at him the entire time he ate. When he got up to leave, someone actually clapped.

Jess caught the other girl's eye, and they both laughed. "Ignorant git," she commented to Jess, who agreed.

"I know, I couldn't believe how inconsiderate he was. He could have just left the cake. He didn't need to say anything."

"You new around here?" the girl asked.

"Yeah, we just moved here a couple of weeks ago," Jess replied.

"Can I sit with you?" Before waiting for an answer, the girl grabbed her stuff and moved over to Jess' table. "I'm Fran. Do you want another drink?" she asked.

"Thanks, I'll have a Coke, and I'm Jess."

Fran chatted as though they'd known each other forever. She told Jess all about the area, what it was like living there, what there was to do, and all the things that weren't available.

"I'm training to be a nursing associate," Fran said proudly.

"What does that mean? I've never heard of it before," Jess said.

"It means I train on the job and I help the nurses. In the future, I could do more training and become a nurse."

"I couldn't do that. I'm too squeamish. Not keen on the sight of blood."

"I don't love it, but you get used to it. You have to." Fran laughed. "The best thing about it is I don't have to go away from home. I'm here to support Mum if she needs me."

"Does she often need support?"

"Yes, she suffers from depression, so having me close helps keep her on an even keel. My sister, Kyra, is in Liverpool. She's a journalist, so she doesn't get home as often as she might. In fact, she only moved back up here earlier this year. She'd been working down in the South West, in a little town called Whittingbury. Loved it, she did, but Mum has been bad over this last year, so when the opportunity of a job came up, Kyra jumped at it. She doesn't have to live with us, which I know she's glad about, but Liverpool isn't that far for her to pop down if Mum and I need her. It's a great support for me."

Jess sat listening, feeling envious that Fran still had her mum. Jess noticed Fran hadn't mentioned a dad. "So, where's your dad?"

"That's the odd bit. Dad lived in Bideford, which is where he was from, and he brought up Kyra, but I've always been with Mum. They split just before I was born. Mum is Jamaican, and she couldn't cope when they were together, because they often got racist comments."

Jess shook her head.

"Does it bother you that I'm mixed?" Fran asked. "Hadn't you guessed?"

She was embarrassed that Fran thought her ethnicity worried her.

"No, I'm sorry. I was surprised, that's all. You just look like you have a slight tan. It hadn't crossed my mind that either of your parents were Jamaican. And, no, it doesn't worry me either way."

Fran smiled. "I'm not upset, but people do react in various ways. I think what upset Mum most, and probably tipped her over the edge, were the cruel things people used to say. When they saw her out with Kyra, they'd stare, as if they couldn't understand why she was with her. Kyra's skin is lighter than hers, so they didn't think she could be Kyra's mum. Dad didn't fully understand, and the more paranoid Mum became, the more their relationship suffered. So, she left him, but by that time, she was pregnant with me, though she didn't tell Dad. In the end, she met someone else, who was my stepdad for a time, and then when I was a teenager, he left Mum too. So, since then it's been me and her. Until the last year when Kyra moved nearer. Our dad died earlier this year."

Fran smiled at Jess again.

Jess was slightly taken aback by how uninhibited Fran was being, in the way that she was talking about her family. But Jess welcomed her openness.

She changed the subject. “So, aren’t you training today?”

“I’ve got a few days off. An uncle of Mum’s passed away, so they’ve given me leave for the funeral and some time to be with Mum.” Fran looked at her mobile and, packing up her stuff, said, “I’d better be going. Do you fancy coming out for a drink tonight? A group of us meet up at the Blue Dolphin when we’re around. If you don’t know anyone, it would be a good place to meet a few other locals.”

“Do you live in this – this village too?” Jess was surprised there might actually be other young people living here.

“No, I live just the other side, under the bridge. It’s not far. So, do you fancy coming along later?”

Jess hesitated. She wasn’t sure how she would feel meeting up with a load of people she didn’t know, but then that was the whole point. She needed to make friends, otherwise she’d be stuck at home until next October, without getting to know anyone. As she agreed to go, the memory of the dark-haired barman popped into her head.

6

About twenty minutes after Jess had left the house, Sally rang Danny back.

"Danny. You were the last person I expected to hear from. How can I help?"

Danny already wished he hadn't rung her.

"Well, it's a bit difficult, but...I know you believe in ghosts and all that sort of stuff."

"The 'woo-woo' stuff is what Kate said you referred to it as," she replied.

"Yes, I'm sorry, but I just can't believe it's real. Anyway, the problem is Jess has been having these terrible nightmares. Dreams where she keeps seeing someone drowning, but it is as though she herself is drowning, and when she wakes up, she's actually wet." Danny paused to think about what else to say.

"She is physically wet?" Sally asked.

"Yes. And," he continued, "she has seen a woman several times in her room, who has spoken to her. Not out loud, but in her head somehow. Jess said that the woman told her she wanted to share her story with her. I think it's all in her—"

"Danny, it sounds as though you have a lost spirit in your house."

This time, Danny interrupted her. "Come on, Sally, don't be silly. You seriously think we have a ghost?"

When Sally replied, it was in a very measured tone. "You rang me to ask me for my advice, because I believe in things you don't, and now you don't want to accept what I'm saying? I think you have a spirit in your home." She paused.

Feeling slightly contrite, Danny said, "I'm sorry, but what can I do? I need to help Jess, because it's wearing her down, and she's hardly sleeping."

"I think the first thing to do is research if anyone has died in your house. Find out about them, and then you might know why they are still in this world when they should have crossed over to the other side."

'The other side', seriously? he thought. "But that won't stop the dreams, will it?"

"No, but it might give you an answer as to why the person is still in this life rather than the afterlife. I'd find out that information before doing anything else."

"Anything else, like what?" Danny asked.

"Like having a spiritual cleanse."

"Is that like an exorcism?"

"Don't be so crass, Danny. We're not talking *The Exorcist*. You need to talk to Jess. She might not want to get rid of her visitor. She might actually want to find out why she's here."

"Sally, why on earth is this happening to Jess?" Danny asked.

There was a long pause before Sally replied. "I think probably, because you are both grieving after Kate's death, and young girls in particular are more susceptible to drawing spirits to them. There must be a reason that this woman hasn't passed to the other side, and she obviously feels some connection to Jess."

"I didn't know that about girls. So, basically, this spirit is sort of tapping into Jess' grief?"

"It could be, but that's why I think you need to do some research to find out who lived in your house, and also talk to Jess."

"Okay, I guess you're right. I'll talk to her. Thank you, Sally. I appreciate you giving me the time."

"That's okay. If you want any more help, I can always drive over to where you are and see if I also feel a presence in the house. And if Jess wants to ask anything, I'm here."

"Thanks again. I'll get in touch and let you know what we find out. Bye."

~

Later, as Jess walked back into the house, she shouted out, "I'm going out with some locals tonight at the Blue Dolphin, at seven thirty, so what time are we having tea?"

Danny didn't reply.

"Dad. Where are you Dad? Dad!"

Walking into the lounge, she found Danny lying on the sofa, an empty glass and bottle of whisky on the floor beside him.

"Dad!" She shook him, and he woke abruptly, a guilty look on his face. He pulled himself up into a sitting position and stretched.

"Are you okay, Dad? You scared me when it was so quiet in the house."

"Sorry. I'm fine. I just needed a bit of a rest and had a little tipple..."

"Mm, so I can see. Drinking in the daytime, that's how it starts."

"Hey, who's the parent here? I needed a drink." Danny looked a little sheepish.

"Did you hear me? I'm going out tonight to meet some locals at the Blue Dolphin."

Danny, whose eyes were more focused than they'd been when he'd first woke, glanced up and gave her an appraising look.

"Who did you meet?"

"A girl, Fran, and she invited me."

"That's good. It'll be good to get to know some people your own age."

After his chat with Sally, Danny had finished off another glass or two of the whisky – trying to gear himself up for when Jess got back from her walk. He had planned to talk to her about his conversation with Sally but now decided to shelve the idea, especially as she seemed in such a good mood. Feeling a little guilty yet quietly relieved, he decided the talk could wait until tomorrow.

"You didn't do much more renovating then," Jess said.

"No, I, er...got sidetracked. There's no rush. It's not like it's going anywhere, and the plumber can't come until next week now." To his surprise, Jess bent down and kissed him on his cheek.

"Do you want help making tea?"

"Well, it's going to have to be something pretty simple. We need to use up stuff that'll go off. How about eggs and beans on toast?"

Jess nodded. It was one of their family favourites when they couldn't be bothered to cook a 'proper meal', as Mum had called it. "I'll do the toast."

Two hours later, there was a knock on the door. Jess bounded down to greet Fran and disappeared off for the evening. She looked brighter than Danny had seen her look for some time, and for the first time in ages, she was wearing a colourful top rather than the dark colours she seemed to have lived in the last few months. He was finding it hard to cope with her mood swings and hoped making a local friend might help her.

With the TV on in the background, for company more than anything, Danny grabbed his laptop and got himself a drink while he left it to boot up. He considered pouring himself another glass of his favourite tipple but decided against it and made himself a coffee before settling down to find out who'd previously lived in the house. After searching on the government's land registry site and paying a small fee, he was able to view the names of past owners online. Luckily, there weren't that many. The first person was an Amy McKenzie, who lived in the house from 1939 to 1958, then Walter and Agnes Owen, until 1997, and latterly, a property company, called Jenkins, who had rented the house out until about a year before he and Jess had moved in. Danny wrote the title 'Previous owners' before writing the names on a piece of paper, leaving a gap between each, where he intended to add more information if he found it. He wanted to be able to show Jess something tangible, rather than having to search online again.

He started to search for registered deaths, hoping that might give him more of a clue to the identity of their 'visitor', but his eyes kept glazing over, and before he knew it, he nodded off, only to be woken when his head suddenly fell forward. Danny hadn't realised how tired the renovation was making him, plus, of course, the whole emotional drain of his loss and dealing with Jess. He shut the laptop and collapsed onto the sofa, where he instantly fell asleep.

Jess and Fran entered the noisy pub, Fran leading the way towards a particularly rowdy group of people all around her age. Although Jess was pretty confident in herself, she was grateful to be with Fran as she was a little hesitant about joining a group where they all knew each other.

"Hi, this is Jess," Fran yelled to the group. Some people looked up, others continued their conversations, but there was a mishmash of voices saying, "Hi".

"My turn to get you a drink. What do you fancy?"

"A cider, please," Fran said.

Jess went to the bar, which was packed, mostly with older men who were hogging the space and chatting despite having already been served with their drinks. She was surprised when a voice asked, "What can I get you?"

It was the guy with the dark, curly hair she'd seen the night she had visited with her dad. He gave her a broad smile as he got the drinks she'd ordered. "With your dad again?" he asked, looking over her shoulder.

"No, with some new friends. The noisy lot over there." She pointed to where Fran and her friends were sitting.

He nodded. "They're always in here on a Friday night before they move on."

The conversation continued with a few jokes as they flirted with each other, and he took far longer than needed to serve her drinks. As he passed them over, he said, "Come and find me when I'm on my break. It'll be in about half an hour." He winked at her as she turned to walk away.

Normally she'd think that was pretty lame, but he was the cutest thing she'd seen since getting here, so she answered over her shoulder. "Maybe."

Fran's friends were a mad lot and soon made Jess feel

welcome. There were about ten of them, plus her and Fran. More guys than girls, but a good crew. Two of the guys were together, which was cool. They weren't quite what she would have expected for Llandreary-u! When she told them her disparaging name for the village, they all had a go at her, though underneath the bravado, they agreed.

She hadn't mentioned to Fran about the guy at the bar, but noticing he was no longer there, she told Fran she was going to the loo.

She went out of the pub's back door, rather than the front entrance, as she guessed that's where he might be. Sure enough, he was standing leaning against the wall, smoking. "I didn't know if you'd come. Do you want one?" He offered Jess a cigarette.

After indicating 'no', she learnt his name was Scott, and he'd lived in Llaneirw his whole life, though he hoped to escape to Liverpool sometime in the future. He knew Jess had just moved here, but she didn't tell him about her mum. He suddenly leant in and kissed her. Jess was surprised but not unhappy about his move. He pulled her in closer, and the second kiss lingered and was much deeper. His hands moved towards her breasts, but she was okay with that. She needed this warmth. As she responded to his kisses and didn't move his wandering hands, Scott pulled her into a darker space behind the door. In fact, this whole side of the pub was less well-lit than the front, and main entrance. She was enjoying his body against hers, his deep lingering kisses, and it was good to be wanted. She hadn't let herself go or had any enjoyment for far too long. Breathing heavily, she relaxed into the moment. He slipped his hands inside her joggers and her panties, and although part of her wanted the feel of his fingers, she tried to pull away.

"No, I don't want to go any further. I don't know you." The spell broke.

"Oh, come on, you're no kid. Didn't you know why I asked you out here? Come on, you know you want it." He pushed her against the wall, pinning her against the hard bricks, and began unzipping his jeans with his free hand.

Jess struggled; he was so much stronger than her. It always annoyed her how easy it was for men to force themselves onto women by pure strength. She tried to push him off while he was pushing his body into hers, trying to pull her joggers down. "Get off me!" Holding on to the top of her panties to keep them up, somehow, she managed to free a leg from his weight, and with all her might, she stamped on the instep of his foot.

Scott let go of her for an instant. He seemed to be in immense pain. Then to add insult to injury, Jess kneed him in the crotch.

Between gasps, he murmured, "You little bitch. You're just a tease."

At that moment, Fran appeared from inside the pub.

"What the hell's going on? I thought you were taking a long time in the loo, Jess."

She instantly took in the situation. "Scott Morgan, you bastard, were you trying it on? I'm going to tell Cerys. I bet this isn't the first time you've gone too far with a customer, is it?"

Jess had managed to get her clothing straightened up and was impressed with Fran's reaction. She was shaking a little, but through anger rather than fear.

"Come on, Jess. Let's get back inside and join the real men around here." Fran grabbed her arm and led her back into the bar, leaving Scott still wincing with the pain of his foot and his manhood.

Jess sat down next to Johnny and Rhys, pleased to see that the others had left already.

"You okay, love?" Rhys asked.

"I'm fine. Fran came along just at the right time."

"Yeah, Scott was up to his old tricks, but he went too far this time. He had the poor girl pinned against the wall."

Johnny and Rhys both gave Jess a look of horror.

"Johnny, get Jess a drink while I'm having a quick word with Cerys." Fran stormed off.

"Did he really 'try it on'? You can only have met him tonight..." Rhys asked.

Johnny interrupted to ask what she'd like to drink, and when she answered, "A cider," he suggested something stronger might be better, and did she like vodka? He disappeared over to the counter.

Rhys and Jess sat in silence. She was grateful when Johnny returned with the vodka. Shortly afterwards, Fran appeared with a woman around the same age as Jess' mum.

"This is Cerys, who runs the pub."

Cerys leant in and spoke to Jess quietly so that no one else around them could hear. "I'm so sorry, love. Are you okay? Do you want to report him to the police?" Cerys asked.

"No, I went out there of my own choice. And, I was quite happy kissing him, but he just took it too far."

"But if he tried to force himself on you, then that is attempted rape, and especially if you told him 'no'."

Jess panicked. She knew Cerys was right, because, technically, Scott had attempted to rape her, but she had happily kissed him and let him grope her. She knew if she hadn't managed to kick him, she might not have stopped him. But, she also knew she couldn't face talking to the police or having them turn up at home. She and her dad had seen enough of the police. Enough to last a lifetime.

"No. I'll not report him, but will you keep an eye on him in the future?"

"I won't be keeping an eye on him. I've just sent him packing. I've had complaints about him before, but no one has ever caught him. Now, I'm worried that he might have got away with it in the past. Annoyingly, he's a good-looking lad, and he knows it, so he thinks he can get away with anything." Cerys put her hand on Jess'. "I hope it won't stop you from coming in here again. I promise you he won't even be allowed near the place."

"Thanks, Cerys. I appreciate that."

Jess finished her vodka. Her new friends tried their best to lighten the mood. The group returned to chatting and eventually joking.

At closing time, Johnny, Rhys and Fran said they'd walk Jess home. Although it was literally no distance at all, she was happy to have some company back to hers.

When they arrived, she apologised for not inviting them in, explaining that the house was a tip. They said it wasn't a problem, and Fran said she'd text her tomorrow, and the three of them disappeared back off towards town.

For the second time that day, Danny was asleep on the sofa when Jess went into the living room. This time, she was relieved, because she really didn't want to have a conversation about the evening, especially after what had happened. His laptop was on the table, with some notes next to it. She took the information which he'd titled, 'Previous owners', deciding she'd have a look herself later. She leant forward and kissed him on his forehead. He opened his eyes, sleepily said, 'Hello, love', and then closed them again, instantly falling back to sleep.

Up in her room, Jess put the notes on her desk and quickly glanced at them. *Great, not too many people we'll have to research.* She sipped from a glass of water and put the glass next to the list.

Jess tried not to think about what had happened earlier, but the memory of Scott forcing her with his strength made her feel sick, thinking about what could have happened. She was so thankful Fran came out when she did. Letting out a long sigh, she tore off her joggers and top, and without bothering to have a wash or clean her teeth, crawled into bed. She fell asleep almost instantly.

The old woman had been watching her. She was sorry that she had so much going on in her young life. She was desperate to find out what had happened to her soulmate, but she needed to be patient. Waiting just that little bit longer wouldn't make that much difference, considering the time she'd been lonely. Although she wanted to continue to share her story with this girl, instead she whispered, *Sleep deeply tonight, my dear.* After running her hand over the girl's hair, she moved over to the desk and stared at the names. A smile spread across her face.

7

Jess had awoken feeling more refreshed. Until she'd remembered what had nearly happened the night before. She felt dirty and needed to shower.

After a good soaking, she emerged feeling much fresher. Walking back into her room, she saw the woman standing by her desk, looking down at the piece of paper where her dad had written the names. She gave Jess a quizzical smile, then disappeared.

Jess walked over to her desk and looked at the list. While she'd slept, her glass of water had somehow spilt over the paper. It had smudged the last two names completely, leaving only the name 'Amy McKenzie' completely legible.

Jess' heart quickened with excitement. This is who the woman must be, and it was her who spilt it. *That's why she was smiling when I walked into the room.*

"Dad, Dad. Where are you?" Jess rushed up to his room and then, finding it empty, rushed downstairs, where she found him in the kitchen. Holding up the soggy piece of paper, she said, "Look, this is the name of the old woman. It must be! It's the only name that didn't get smudged. There was even water all around the piece of paper. And I saw her this morning, standing by the desk."

Danny started to say something, but Jess interrupted before he even got a word out of his mouth.

"I know you're going to say she's a figment of my imagination, but I did see her, and she smiled at me like she was dead pleased with herself." Jess laughed at her unintended joke before continuing. "Anyway, if I'd have knocked the water over it would have obliterated all the names."

Danny was quiet for a moment. "Well, I have to admit, it is odd that only that name didn't get smudged." He sighed. "Okay. We'll see what we can find."

Jess smiled at him and made herself a coffee.

"Did you have a good time with your new friend – Ann? Oh, and by the way, I spoke to your mum's friend Sally last night while you were out."

Not wanting to say much about the night before, and surprised he'd phone Sally, Jess focused on that. "I had a good time with Fran, not 'Ann' – thanks. Why were you speaking to Sally? I didn't think you two liked each other."

"Well, we're not best buddies, no. I just thought...erm, you know, her being a bit 'woo-woo', she might have some ideas about what's been going on. With you seeing the apparition of this woman."

"Thanks, Dad. Talk about me behind my back, why don't you?" She tried not to get too peeved, especially after he'd found a possible name for her woman.

"Was she helpful?"

"Actually, she was. She's the reason I looked up previous owners last night. She suggested if we found out who had lived here, and if someone might have died in the house, we might know who it is you keep seeing."

"So, because Sally tells you that, you suddenly believe her, but when I tell you, I'm imagining things. Right?"

"Er...Not really. I'm trying to keep an open mind."

Jess laughed. "You liar. I know you don't believe me. But at least you've helped."

Danny opened his laptop, and together, he and Jess searched for Amy McKenzie's name in the list of deaths for the year 1958, in Llaneirw. Fairly quickly, they found that she had died in their house at the age of 74, with her previous occupation being seamstress and bookkeeper. Jess suddenly burst into tears.

Danny hugged her close. "Love, you're okay. What are you crying for? Now you know who your lady is."

"I know, they're happy tears. Now I can connect with her more and try to find out why she is here." She wiped her eyes. "Let's Google her and see if there is anything about her."

"You do it. You're better at searching than me."

Jess swapped places with her dad and typed in Amy's name, 'Llaneirw' and 'drowning'. While she searched, Danny went to make another cup of coffee for them both. "Dad, you won't believe this. I've just found an old newspaper article about a ship called the *Aliciana* sinking in 1915."

"Go on, tell me about it." He sipped his coffee then placed the mug on the table.

"Well, it says here that the *Aliciana* was a passenger ship sailing to Liverpool from the US, and it was torpedoed off the Welsh coastline by a U-boat. Twelve hundred people were either drowned or killed in the disaster. It seems that Amy was a survivor, and after recovering, she moved to Llaneirw to live, because her husband was presumed drowned, but his body was never recovered and she wanted to be beside the sea!" Jess took a swig of her coffee. "God, can you imagine she survived and he died?"

After what seemed a long moment of silence, Danny answered. “Yes, sadly, I can.”

Jess looked at him, her eyes refilling with tears. “Oh, God, I’m sorry, Dad. That was thoughtless of me. It just came out.”

“Don’t be silly, love. I know you didn’t mean anything. Anyway, you know, I can’t imagine wanting to look at the place where the person I loved died. That’s why we’re here. What else does it say about Amy?”

Jess focused back on the screen. “Erm...hang on...She moved here from Manchester where her husband William’s family had cared for her after the disaster. She lived with them for quite a while but then wanted to be near him. Most of the rest of the article is her talking about the actual sinking and how she was saved. I’ve seen some of this in my dreams, but I might read it again sometime, just not now.”

Jess closed the laptop. “I think we’ll have to see if we can find out more about them online, plus there might be something in the library about the sinking, if it happened on this coastline.”

“I think your mum joined that Ancestry site a while before she...” He took another sip of his coffee. “I can guess her password. I’ll have a go to see if I can get online, and we’ll see what we can find on there too.”

“Thanks, Dad. I know you were beginning to think I was mad, but at least now you know Amy is, or was, real.” Jess put her arms around her dad’s neck and hugged him. It was the first time for ages that they’d been so connected.

Jess’ mobile rang, interrupting the moment. She quickly glanced to see who it was. Fran, probably ringing to check she was okay after last night.

“Sorry, it’s Fran. I’d better pick up. Maybe if she’s free on Monday, she could come to the library with me. At least she’ll know where it is.”

Fran had agreed to meet Jess at the end of the walkway under the main road and then they could walk to the library together. Despite Jess' ordeal on the Friday night, she walked with a spring in her step. Jess couldn't explain fast enough what had happened, telling Fran all about Amy and how she'd lived in their house, and the sinking. Although, at this point, she didn't mention that Amy was a ghost. She made up a story about finding something belonging to her while they were renovating.

The small, serious, bespectacled woman, who was Jess' exact image of a librarian, was far more helpful than she'd ever hoped for, aiming them towards some local books about the disaster. She also gave Jess some online links to passenger lists for the *Aliciana*. They typed the link into Google and asked the librarian if they could print what they found. She also suggested they visit the university library in Bangor as they might have even more information. Incredibly, she was also able to tell Jess that Amy was buried in St Eirw's church, which was the one in their cul-de-sac. She would definitely make time to visit the churchyard and find her grave.

After thanking the librarian, Jess and Fran took the opportunity to check out the passenger list she'd printed off for them for the *Aliciana* on the date of the sinking. It didn't take long to find Amy McKenzie, and next to her name, that of her husband William. A shiver went through Jess' body when she read his name. This was the love of Amy's life, and Jess now realised, the name she'd called out in her panic as the ship had started to sink.

When they'd finished, Jess asked Fran when she would have to go back to work. Fran told her, "The day after next," but she said they could catch up tonight, if Jess wanted.

"Do you mind coming round to mine, rather than us go out? I want you to see where we live and also tell you more about Amy. Can you grab a bottle of wine on your way? I'll pay you for it."

"Okay, that sounds cool. What time do you want me?"

"Around eight. Is that okay?"

Fran nodded, saying, "Give us a *cwtch*."

"A what?"

"It's Welsh for 'hug'." Fran laughed and hugged Jess, who bounded away from the library with the same energy she'd had when she arrived.

Over their takeaway, Jess told Danny about all the information they'd found. As they finished eating, Jess' phone rang. She ran out of the room when she saw the number.

"Hi, Lukas, how was it then?"

"It was amazing. Far better than I'd hoped, and Mum took us to visit some of her relatives in Kalmar. We even managed to go and visit Vaxholm, the town where my great-grandfather came from. Though we didn't have time to search out any of his relatives, but at least I've seen where Dad's family come from," Lukas answered.

"Can't wait to hear all about it when I get to see you," Jess replied, trying to sound casual and not pushy.

"So, how is it all going in the new house? Are you settling in okay?" Lukas asked.

Jess didn't want to tell him about what had been going on, so lied, telling him it was "all good".

"I'm hoping to come down to visit Grandfather in a few weeks – well at least before Christmas. I wondered if you'd fancy coming with me. He lives on Anglesey. What do you think?"

Jess silently did a little happy dance around her room. Calming herself down, she tried to sound cool about it. "Yeah, that'd be great. I'm sure Dad will be pleased to be rid of me for a bit. I'll check with him." She suddenly caught sight of the time. "Sorry, gotta go, I've got a girlfriend coming over."

"You've not wasted time making new friends then. Okay, I'll ring soon to arrange things. *Hejdå*." Then he added. "Oh, sorry, it's 'goodbye' in Swedish."

"Bye," Jess said, smiling to herself. From anyone else, it would have sounded pretentious, but somehow, coming from him, it just sounded sexy. Jess ran downstairs almost taking two at a time.

"Was that who I think it was?" Danny asked.

"Yep. He's back from Sweden, and he's going to take me to Anglesey when he goes over to see his grandfather. You don't mind, do you?"

"No. It'll do you good to get away from me banging around in the house. When?"

"Probably the end of this month."

"That's fine. Hopefully by then we'll have a decent kitchen and downstairs for him to see."

Danny smiled at Jess, who was bounding around the room in a much happier mood than he'd seen for months. He was glad Lukas had got in touch. It had been so long since the funeral, which was the last time they'd been in contact. Danny was beginning to worry that he'd lost interest. It was obvious she was keen on Lukas, just by the way she lit up whenever his name was mentioned, so Danny was relieved that perhaps the feelings were reciprocated.

However, boys, or men, was a subject Danny worried about. He didn't have a clue what he was going to say when she brought someone home. There was no way he could have conversations about the finer details of sex, which he knew Kate would have done, and easily. Thank goodness Kate had been there when she'd started menstruating, and that she had talked to Jess about contraception when she'd joined the sixth form. The doorbell interrupted Danny's self-deprecation of his relationship advice. Being the nearest to the front door, he opened it to see a young, dark-haired girl beaming up at him.

"Hi, I'm Fran,"

"Come in. Jess is around."

In fact, Jess was standing behind him. She grabbed Fran by the hand and led her into the lounge, which was still an unfinished kitchen-cum-living space, but at least it was now cleared of the old kitchen altogether. Danny followed on behind.

"I'll make us a coffee and grab some glasses too for our wine." Jess nodded towards the bottle Fran held in her right hand. Then with a fair amount of sarcasm asked, "What do you think of Dad's handiwork?"

Danny looked at Fran, putting her on the spot.

"Er. It's different."

He laughed, knowing she was trying to be polite. "Yes, that's certainly a description. 'Different' is the word. It will be finished, hopefully, over the next few weeks. Hopefully in time for Christmas."

Jess handed two glasses to Fran to carry, along with the bottle of wine, while she carried the two cups of coffee. "See you later, Dad. We'll leave you to it."

Up in Jess' room, Fran said, "Wow, I love the colours." She gazed around the room. "It's brilliant. And you've got a view of the sea." Putting the wine and glasses down on the desk, she took her coffee from Jess. "The house is going to look great when your dad has finished."

Jess nodded. "He needs something to keep him busy, so it could take some time."

"Do you mind if I look around?" Fran asked. Again, Jess nodded and sat on her bed. Fran browsed through Jess' books then looked at the artwork she had on her wall, and lastly, she noticed the photograph on the desk. “Is that your mum?”

Another nod from Jess. She didn’t add anything, and Fran didn’t ask more.

“I’ve just had a call from Lukas, a friend I met when I went to Manchester for my uni interview last year. I haven’t spoken to him since...” She paused. “Since February. He’s just got back from Sweden, and he’s going to take me to Anglesey in a couple of weeks. His grandad lives there.”

“You two gotta thing going on, then?” Fran asked.

“No. No, we’re just friends at the moment. But, he’s so hot. He’s got this gorgeous mop of thick, blond hair, and the bluest of eyes.” Jess smiled at Fran. “And an incredibly fit body to match.”

“Well, good luck keeping your hands off him then.”

“Not very likely. We’re going to his grandad’s,” Jess said.

“You never know. Anyway, maybe his grandad’s deaf.” Fran gave her a knowing look. “Mind you, it depends how noisy you are?”

They both laughed.

Having opened the wine, they’d downed several glasses and had begun to share stories about their conquests. Fran said she’d been surprised Jess hadn’t been more upset about the incident with Scott. But Jess had told her about some of the boys she’d met in Liverpool and had reassured her that she knew how to take care of herself and wasn’t quite as innocent as she appeared.

Several wines later, Jess asked Fran if she believed in ghosts.

“As it happens, yes I do. I saw one in our old house once, but not since we moved. Why?”

Sensing that Fran wouldn’t laugh at her, Jess told her about Amy and how she’d been visiting her in her dreams, which was why they’d been to the library.

"Now I understand why you were so excited about the information we found. What else have you found out?"

"We've got her husband's name, Will, and when he died, but I still don't know why she's still here. That's what I've got to find out next," Jess answered.

"I'm happy to help if you want me to. And I can ask Kyra where we can look for things. She should know."

"That'd be great. Thanks, Fran."

Fran left around 11.00 p.m., saying that this would be her last late week-night for some time as she had to go back to her training next week. She promised to text Jess.

Danny shouted "Goodbye" as Fran left, and, kissing Jess goodnight, went to bed to read.

Entering her room, Jess saw Amy standing near the end of her bed, pointing to the carpet. Jess bent down to take a look but couldn't see anything. Amy looked agitated but didn't seem able to explain why she wanted Jess to look at that spot in the room.

"I'll get Dad to have a look in the morning, Amy."

Jess received the most wonderful smile in recognition of using Amy's name.

You know who I am!

Jess smiled back. "And I know that Will was your husband. Is that why you're still here?"

Amy nodded, then vanished.

Jess was surprised by her sudden disappearance. She'd expected Amy to ask questions, or tell her more.

Waiting for Amy to reappear and going over all the information she and Fran had found, Jess didn't expect to get much sleep that night.

But Amy hadn't shared any dreams with Jess that night. However, when she'd woken up, in the stillness of the morning air, Amy had appeared in the same spot she'd stood the night before, pointing to the carpet.

While eating breakfast with Danny, Jess asked for a favour. "Dad, do you think you could check something for me?"

"Depends." Danny had his head in the book he was reading. Jess didn't take much notice of what it was.

"Well, Amy..."

"Amy who?" Danny asked, absentmindedly.

"Amy the ghost. Dad, concentrate. She keeps pointing to a spot on the floor in my room. Do you think you can lift the carpet? Pretty please."

Danny glanced up at her, sighed, and put his book down. "Okay, come on. Show me."

They went into Jess' room, and she indicated the spot where Amy had pointed. Danny had to move some of Jess' stuff so that he could get the corner of the carpet up. He eventually managed to peel it back and pull up the underlay. Beneath that was another layer of thin wool carpet and even older underlay.

"For goodness' sake. Why do people do things by halves?" Danny yanked the old underlay back, letting loose a load of dust as the older, hessian underlay crumbled into a greying mass. Below that, the wooden floorboards were exposed.

"What can you see?" Jess asked, trying hard to get close enough to see for herself.

"Hang on, love. I need to pull this back a little further so I can shine a light on the floorboards. Can you move those boxes?" he asked, pointing to some boxes full of books.

Pulling and shoving with her feet, Jess managed to move them, while Danny exposed more of the wooden boards.

"Pass my torch, can you? I'll have a look to see if anything has fallen underneath them." He shone the light over the boards into the cracks, some of which were large enough for small objects to easily fall between.

Something glistened as the torchlight fell on it. "What's that?" Jess pointed towards where she'd seen the glinting object. Danny shone the torch in that area again.

They were both excited to see what it was. It had looked like a piece of jewellery.

"I've got a strong magnet downstairs," Danny said. "I'll get it and see if I can get the object out without having to take up the floorboards."

Jess held her breath as he rushed downstairs and back up, immediately getting to work with the magnet.

Whatever Danny did, he couldn't attract the jewellery to the magnet. "It must be gold. I remember reading somewhere that real gold isn't attracted to a magnet, though I don't remember why."

Danny stopped and thought for a while and then ran downstairs again. He returned with an old, thin rasp file that he managed to get in between the floorboards. After a great deal of manoeuvring, he managed to get the rasp at an angle where he could wiggle it underneath the chain of what looked like some kind of necklace. Slowly, with great care, he pulled it free. Danny held his hand out for Jess to take the object from him.

Although in need of a clean, it was still recognisable as a beautiful, gold pendant.

Jess gasped. "Do you think it's Amy's? I think it is. I think that's why she's been pointing at the space."

"Open it then. Look inside," Danny said, seeming to be as intrigued as Jess.

Carefully, Jess opened the locket, and there inside was a

photo of a young woman who she instantly recognised as Amy. On the other side was a photo and a lock of hair.

"Is it Amy?" Danny asked.

Jess nodded.

"Do you think that's William?" Danny asked, and at the same time, Jess said, "That must be Will."

"Thank you, Dad, that's incredible. Now I know what Will looks like and I can find out more about him. This is so exciting!" Jess hugged and kissed her dad, who was trying to push the carpet back into place but lost his patience.

"I'll leave it like this for now, but I'll take it up properly another time."

Danny went down to continue his work in the kitchen and Jess sat in her room gazing at the pendant. She opened it up again and then found she could open up the side where the small lock of hair lay across the photo.

Jess looked closely at the photo of Will. He was handsome, in an old-fashioned way. He had very dark hair, a good moustache that wouldn't have looked out of place now, and dark smiling eyes. Out loud, seemingly to no one in particular, but in case Amy was there watching, Jess said, "I'm not surprised you fell for him."

She wondered if she should wear it. Would Amy mind? She decided, probably not, otherwise, why show it to her? Besides, it stood less chance of being lost if she wore it. She grabbed a tissue and gently rubbed the locket, removing the dust of years of being hidden in the floor. After tying her long hair up in a clip, Jess checked that the clasp was sturdy, undid it, and hung the locket around her neck. Looking at herself in the mirror, Jess decided it looked good.

Feeling confident and focused, Jess set off to the library to do some more research and find what she could about Will McKenzie. But before she left the cul-de-sac, she walked over to the churchyard. As luck would have it, there was someone tending graves, so Jess approached him to ask if he could point her in the right direction. The old gardener said he knew the area where she might find people who were buried in the late 1950s. Jess wandered over to where he'd pointed and started walking between the gravestones, reading the names. Just when she was about to give up, she found the grave.

Amy McKenzie 1884–1958.
Loving wife of Will McKenzie.
Reunited at last.

The grave was pretty untidy, which is why she nearly missed it. It appeared no one had visited it for many years, if not decades. She knelt and cleared away some of the weeds and leaves that had blown and settled around the stone cross. Jess knelt back on her heels and looked around to see where the gardener was. He was far away on the other side of the graveyard, so she spoke to Amy. "I wanted to ask you if you're okay with me wearing your locket?"

A gentle breeze appeared from nowhere, and she heard Amy's voice. *Yes, as long as you care for it. You are the bearer of our story, now, Jess. You hold both of our hearts. Keep it safe.*

The chill disappeared as quickly as it had arrived, and Jess was alone, apart from the gardener, who was now moving her way. She touched the locket, and in her head, said, *I promise, I am going to find out what happened to Will.* She walked out of the churchyard and wandered under the bridge towards the local library.

During her trip to the library, she discovered that Will had been born in Scotland before moving to Manchester with his parents when he was four years old. There was a small reference to him in a newspaper from 1915, about the sinking of the *Aliciana*, where it spoke of William McKenzie, carpenter, returning to his native England, because work was scarce in Chicago, due to a strike which had halted building construction. Apart from that, she couldn't find much information at all. She was disappointed, but at least now was certain that this was Amy's husband. Also, she understood why they were leaving Chicago. Having considered the situation further, she appreciated that because Will drowned in the sinking, there wouldn't be any photos of him since that time, and even if he and Amy had brought photos with them, they would have been lost in the disaster.

She thought about her mum's photo sitting on her desk and was grateful that she had loads of images of her mum, even on her mobile phone. The idea of living in a time when you couldn't capture everyday events in photos seemed unimaginable.

Jess continued wearing Amy's locket, although she took it off when she went to bed, scared that it might get tangled in her long hair and break. She placed the locket carefully on her bedside table.

Later that night, Jess woke suddenly in a cold sweat with a searing pain in her side. All she could remember of the dream was seeing a face, close to hers, saying, "You shouldn't stick your nose into other people's business, Mr McKenzie." Suddenly, she felt a sharp pain as the man punched Will in the side.

Sitting up in bed, she switched on her bedside light. It was painful even stretching out for the light switch. Shocked, she realised that she'd seen and experienced Will being attacked. It took a while for her to catch her breath and calm herself.

She got out of bed and walked over to her mirror. Pulling up her top, she saw, just below her ribcage, on the left side of her body, a massive bruise.

She went into the bathroom for a drink of water and then returned to her room, wincing at each movement. She crawled back into bed. Not wanting to fall asleep again, she tried to read the chic-lit that she'd started, but couldn't concentrate. All she could think of was Will and the fact she'd just relived him being attacked. But why would anyone want to harm him? Maybe he hadn't just drowned.

8

LLANEIRW, NOVEMBER 2018

Danny knew the next few weeks were going to be frenetic. Thanks to Paul next door, he had contacted a few tradesmen, who would help him with plumbing and electrical work to ensure that, by the beginning of December, the kitchen would be fitted, leaving only the floor needing to be laid. Maybe the downstairs of the house would be ready by Christmas.

Oh, God! Christmas terrified him. He wasn't sure he was ready for the first Christmas without Kate. They'd always made a big thing of celebrating together as a threesome on Christmas Day and then spending time with friends and relatives for the rest of the holiday season. He hadn't dared ask Jess what she wanted to do.

In fact, it seemed as if the pair of them were ignoring the fact they were only a month away from the big event. Although he hadn't mentioned it to Jess, Kate's parents had invited them to spend Christmas with them in Liverpool, but Danny knew he couldn't face that. As good as the relationship was between them, he couldn't face seeing Kate's mum, a vivid reminder of the fact he would never see Kate at that age. He hoped that his sister-in-law Susie would ask her parents over to stay with her family. He'd almost contacted Susie to ask her to do just that, but decided against it, realising she might not understand where he was coming from. They'd never really seen eye to eye.

On the other hand, Jess was focusing on her trip to Anglesey. So rather than face the dilemma, Danny pushed it to the back of his mind, knowing he would have plenty to keep himself busy with while Jess was away.

Earlier, he had heard her upstairs, bumping stuff around in her room, probably packing, ready for her trip with Lukas. But things had been quiet for a while, so he decided she was probably reading. He cleared away what he was working on, cleaned himself up, and started to prepare dinner.

Jess was actually thinking about her recent dreams. She had dreamt about Will a few more times. The last dream had been so vivid, she couldn't forget it, and the bruise on her side was still faintly visible. Often, she came across Amy in her room, leaning against the wall, looking out to sea. Amy appeared to be calmer than she'd been in the last few months, and Jess decided it was because Amy knew she and Fran had found out more about Will's death. Jess had taken to talking out loud, hoping that Amy was listening, because she wasn't always sure whether she was there or not, as Amy hadn't spoken to her for a while.

Her dad was clattering around downstairs, so she continued packing. Remembering one of her favourite tops was in the ironing pile, she rushed back down, only to find it completely crumpled. She couldn't be bothered to iron it now, so turned to go back upstairs and bumped into her dad, who was looking for her.

"Are you all packed for tomorrow?"

"Nearly. I can't decide what to take with me. Do you think I should take something smart?"

"Probably, just in case. Do you know if you're likely to be going anywhere special while you're there?" Danny asked.

"I don't know. Lukas just told me to pack some warm clothes and some good walking shoes. He didn't mention anything else." She paused halfway up the stairs. "Maybe I'll put in a dress, just in case." She ran back up to her room.

An hour later, Jess reappeared, smelling the food that had just arrived. "As much as I love takeaway, I'm looking forward to when we can cook our own meal again."

"You mean until I can cook for you again? I didn't realise you love my cooking so much." He laughed.

They ate in silence for quite a while, then, in between mouthfuls, unable to look at her dad, Jess asked, "What are we going to do for Christmas?"

Silence returned. Neither of them looked up from their plates.

"Er...I've been wondering the same thing," Danny replied.

She'd caught him out; he wasn't ready for this conversation.

"Do you want to do anything? I mean, do you want to stay here, or go visit someone?"

Again, silence.

"I think." Jess took a breath. "I think we should be together. Just you and me and"—she flicked her eyes towards her dad—"and our memories."

She quickly looked back down at her food. Although she was enjoying it, she was shoving it around the plate with her fork.

Danny looked up and saw a single tear slide down Jess' cheek. He put his fork down and went over to his daughter and hugged her towards him. "That'd be perfect, love."

He kissed her, surreptitiously wiping a tear from his own eyes, as he walked back to finish his meal.

When they finished, Jess cleared away their plates and disposed of the packaging their meal had come in. Danny searched and found the particular CD he'd been looking for. Smiling to himself, he thought, if nothing else, this would lighten the mood. While 'Jump Around' blared out around the house, he started doing a type of bunny hop across the room towards Jess, who had apparently turned around to see what was going on. Despite the recent moment of sadness, it seemed she also couldn't restrain herself. Soon the pair of them were bunny-hopping around together. By the time the track finished, they were both helplessly laughing and short of breath after their exertion. Putting on a faux French accent, Danny said, "Pepé Le Pew strikes again."

When Jess was younger, Danny had introduced her to the Looney Tunes character and would hop around like Pepé to make her laugh. Then, when she became a teenager, Danny introduced her to 'Jump Around' by House of Pain, and the jumping had turned into the Pepé Hop. It had always worked then, as it had now. They hugged, holding each other close for some time.

Jess pulled away, saying, "I need to finish off clearing up."

Feeling energised, Danny sat down to read his book.

Having cleared up, Jess walked over to Danny, who was completely engrossed in his book. She kissed him before going up to her room. "I'm going to finish packing and get my beauty sleep ready for tomorrow."

"I'm sure Lukas thinks you're beautiful enough."

In her room, Jess checked that she had everything she wanted to take with her to Anglesey before texting Fran to say she'd be in touch when she got back. She received a text back from Fran, reminding her to make sure she was ready, if he 'pounced'. *I should be so lucky.*

Waking abruptly, Jess looked at her clock. It was only 5.00 a.m. She was bereft but didn't know why. She shut her eyes, trying to remember what it was she'd been dreaming about. The memory suddenly flooded back into her mind. Through Will's eyes, she had experienced Amy breaking the news to him that she was quite sure now that she was expecting a baby. Jess had felt his excitement and joy at the news, and the love that radiated between them. She had experienced the warmth of their lips, as though she were being kissed too.

"You've made me the happiest man alive, Amy. When we go up for afternoon tea, I'm going to send a telegram to the family with the good news, so they can come and meet us in Liverpool."

This happy scenario had moved into the same dreadful nightmare Jess had previously dreamt. Where the man was telling Will in no uncertain terms to keep his nose out of his business – and again, the sharp pain appeared in her side when the man had suddenly attacked Will, punching him.

What on earth had Will witnessed?

Jess pulled up her top to see if the bruise had returned. It had, looking darker and feeling more painful than before. But there was also another, more visceral, deep sadness because now she knew that Amy must have lost her baby. Her own tears fell. Without having any idea of what it felt to be pregnant, she could fully empathise with Amy. She knew Amy's anguish. This had been their first and last chance to have a family. Amy had suffered two losses, not just one.

"I'm so sorry, Amy. You were pregnant, that's so sad," she said aloud to the empty room, hoping that Amy was there in the shadows, listening.

~

Amy was listening and knew that Jess had been suffering, first with the images she'd shown her, through her dreams of the sinking ship. And, now, although Amy hadn't seen the dreams about Will, she had witnessed the terrible effect they'd taken on Jess.

Amy wanted her to understand the depth of the love they'd shared, so over the next few nights, she invaded Jess' dreams with stories of how they'd met and how they'd lived, hoping that Jess would understand why she'd remained in this plane for such a long time. Now Jess would experience the desperation she had suffered at not finding her soulmate, as she had expected, after her death.

9
MANCHESTER, 1908

Busy selecting material and other haberdashery products, Amy was in the office when Beryl, the shop girl, told her she was just nipping out on an errand. Not long after she'd left, Amy heard the shop bell 'ting', so she put her pen aside and went to serve. A slim, dark-haired young man stood just inside the doorway, looking very uncomfortable, seeming undecided whether to enter or not.

"Can I help you, sir?" Amy asked. He smiled a radiant smile that lit up the entire space and Amy blushed, guilty at having been caught out thinking how handsome he was.

Seemingly not noticing, the young man said, "Thank you, yes. My sister is a seamstress and I'm looking for something special that she could use when dressmaking. She makes all of her own clothes, and they look beautiful."

Amy also made her own clothes. Working in the shop, she was aware of the latest fashions and decided that lace would be the safest thing to suggest to him. After telling him this, he asked to see what they had in stock.

The counter was soon covered in different options, and as she showed him the different patterns, they both went to pick up the same lace. Their hands touched, and it was as though an electric shock had hit Amy's whole being. She snatched her hand away, feeling embarrassed and rather unsettled.

"I do apologise. We obviously both have good taste." He flashed another of his beautiful smiles at her, causing her to become flustered once again.

Lifting the lace, he asked, "How much is this? And how much do you think I'd need to buy her for it to be useful?"

Appearing to be busy working out the cost and amount he should buy, Amy managed to calm herself until she was ready to inform him. He agreed to the sale, and she packaged the lace, carefully tying it with a piece of ribbon.

"Thank you for your help. I know my sister Molly will love it. And thank you for the lovely wrapping – I'm not good at that, so I can give it to her exactly how you've packaged it. Beautifully."

He walked out of the shop then turned and paused. "Good day, miss." He smiled and tipped his hat.

After he'd left, Amy remained standing at the till, in a daze, remembering his dark eyes that sparkled when he smiled. Beryl broke the spell, pushing the door open and barging in like a bull in a china shop.

~

A few weeks later, Amy was busy checking sales figures. She heard the shop bell, followed by Beryl loudly chatting away. She burst into the back room.

"There's a gentleman out here who wants to see you. He said you served him the other week when he bought a present for his sister, Molly."

Amy hurriedly stood up, straightening her skirt and checking her hair was still in place. Beryl gave her a quizzical look.

"Thank you, Beryl. I'll deal with the gentleman."

Bearing a confidence that she didn't feel, she walked into the shop. Waiting, he smiled at her and removed his hat. "Good afternoon."

"Good afternoon, sir. How are you?"

"I am very well, thank you. I wanted to thank you for your help in choosing my sister's present. Molly loved the lace." He paused, looking uncertain about what to say next.

"Erm, I thought I might buy her some buttons today. What do you think?" He smiled.

Again, Amy's heart quivered under the intensity of his glance. Certain she was blushing, she quickly looked away. "What would they be for?" she asked.

"Ah, that's a good question." He paused again. "Erm, do you have some that could perhaps go on any garment?"

"Well, the size of button and the colour of material would be useful to know, to make a choice. But, I wonder, if you bought her some very pretty buttons, she might then make something to go with them!" Amy answered.

This reply initiated another of his smiles. "That's a wonderful idea. Please, show me what you have."

Amy went to the button drawer and chose sets that she would buy herself, if she had the extra money. She placed them on the counter. The first were delicate mother-of-pearl in the shape of small flowers, containing five petals. In the second set, each button was a type of spinning top made from glass, in black and gold. The third were small, round glass sunflowers.

"What do you think of these?" Amy asked.

He looked a little confused, and in the end, asked her which she preferred. Amy smiled back at him and told him her favourites were the mother-of-pearl buttons.

"Then, I will take those. I am sure Molly will like them, if you do."

Amy wrapped them for him, again taking care to make the

package look pretty. As he took them from her, their hands glanced against each other, and yet again, the shock of his touch ran through Amy's body.

He went to go, but as he reached the door, he turned. "May I ask your name? Miss?"

Amy raised her eyebrows and he quickly added, "So I can ask for you by name in the future."

"Of course. Miss Amy Baker. And your name, sir – if I may ask?"

"Mr William McKenzie. Well, good day, Miss Amy Baker." Tipping his hat, he left the shop.

For weeks, Amy had spent her time whispering his name to herself and hoping that he would visit the shop soon. Eventually, when she'd almost given up on seeing him again, he had visited the shop late one Friday afternoon. He invited her to go along with him, his younger sister Molly and her fiancé George, to visit the newly opened Whitworth Institute and Park on the following Sunday afternoon. Will made a point of saying that everything would be perfectly proper, because they would have chaperones. Amy had tried not to sound too keen and took her time to say that she would be delighted.

On the day they'd met, Amy had been thrilled to see Molly wearing a blouse adorned with the buttons William had bought from her. He was right; his sister was a wonderful seamstress.

Over the following weeks, Amy and Will, as he preferred to be called, continued to meet, their affection growing with each hour they spent together. They often walked around Whitworth Institute Park. It was so beautiful, and also easy for them both to reach on the tram. Then, after some time, Molly and George would arrive with Will, but they'd go off on their own, leaving Will and Amy to themselves.

Eventually, Will invited Amy to tea so she could meet the rest of his family, which was a similar size to her own. He had six siblings: five sisters and an older brother. Whereas Amy had seven: five sisters and two brothers. Will and three of his siblings had been born in Dingwall, Ross-shire, but then the family had moved to Manchester.

Both sets of parents were happy with their match. Amy knew her parents were beginning to think she'd end up a spinster, so they were overjoyed when she met Will.

One afternoon, Amy was sitting in the parlour reading when there was a knock at the door. One of her brothers went to answer, and on hearing Will's voice, she was about to rush into the hall to greet him, but heard him ask to speak to her father. Amy sat down and tried to read her book, though she couldn't concentrate on one single word. Her mother kept glancing over at her, smiling.

Amy's stomach was a-flutter with excited nerves. She could hardly remain seated but forced herself to do so, turning pages, pretending to read. Her father came into the room and asked her mother and the other family members present to join him in the kitchen. As everyone else left the room, Will entered. He looked nervous too, but rushed over to Amy. Hardly waiting for her to put her book down, he took her hands and pulled her into a standing position.

"I've just spoken to your father...to ask him if I could ask for your hand in—"

"Yes. I will."

They both burst out laughing, and Will pulled her into his arms and kissed her on the lips.

"I didn't think you'd say no, but I was a little nervous, in case I was wrong," Will said, kissing her again.

Amy touched his face, and pulling away from his lips, said, "I can't wait to be Mrs McKenzie and spend my whole life with you." They kissed again and were finally interrupted by a light knock on the door, as the Baker family piled back into the room to congratulate them both.

In marriage terms, neither of them were youngsters, so rather than wait, they decided to get married as soon as they could. However, Will had always had his heart set on emigrating to America. Initially, when he first told her about it, Amy was heart-broken, thinking that their relationship would end. But when Will showed her how much he could earn as a master-carpenter, and pictures of the city of Chicago – the growing, modern metropolis where he was hoping to work – his gentle persuasion changed her mind.

The time for Will to leave came around all too soon. In March 1909, Will said goodbye, assuring Amy that he'd regularly inform her how he was getting on. He sailed to New York on the Lusitania. A week later, after travelling by rail to Chicago, he set out to find somewhere for them to live, having already secured a job before he left Manchester. He promised to come back as soon as he could so they could marry. They'd talked about having children, and as Amy was already past the age most women had their first babies, they didn't want to wait too long before getting wed.

Will enjoyed his work in Chicago. As the city was growing fast, all types of tradesmen were needed, particularly good carpenters. He found a room in a lodging house, along with two other Scotsmen who had also sailed on the Lusitania, at 4617 Evans Avenue, Cook, Chicago. Things worked a little differently in the US when it came to lodging. Will said he was lucky, though, as the owner of the house was also a Scot, so he and the other boarders were made very welcome. They ate their food all together, like one large family, so in many ways, it was like a home from home. The obvious difference being that, initially, he shared a room with one of the other boarders, and they all shared bathroom facilities.

Amy and Will were apart for nearly two years, and whenever she received the letters written in his hand, she would excitedly rip open the envelope to read his latest news. She would write back straight away, knowing that as soon as he received her letter, he would reply again.

During their time apart, each of them saved as hard as they could. Amy couldn't believe it when Will told her to start planning the wedding, because he had already asked his father to book the church after first secretly writing to her father for his renewed blessing.

Will's boss was unbelievably understanding and gave him time off to return to England and marry. Leaving New York on April 22nd, Will arrived in Liverpool on May 1st. With little time to do much apart from prepare for their marriage and their return to America, their wedding was a fairly small affair, with just close family. They married on Saturday 13th May. They kept the cost down so they could save money for when it would be needed most – settling into a place of their own, back in Chicago.

Molly made Amy's stunning wedding dress, proving again her expert seamstress skills. Feeling beautiful in her bridal gown, Amy carried a small bouquet of a mixture of white and pink roses.

As she walked down the aisle towards Will on their wedding day, Amy was the happiest she'd ever been, and she knew by the look in his eyes, he felt the same.

After their wedding, they didn't have much time to spend

with either of their families. Amy barely had time to consider the fact she was moving to another country, thousands of miles away, the following Saturday.

On May 20th, they boarded the SS Baltic to travel to America, ready to start their new life in the New World.

10
JOURNEY TO CHICAGO, 1911

Amy had never set foot on a ship before, let alone spent eight days at sea. The journey had not been as bad as she'd expected, although she found it a strange sensation when there was no land visible. Several times, Will found her looking over the ship's side, staring into the dark waters far below as it carved its way through the depths towards their new life. Each time, he pulled her close into his arms to warm her, to help her feel safe. But she always enjoyed the bracing sea air as she and Will walked along the deck in the early evenings after their dinner.

However, the part of their journey Amy had found absolutely terrifying was when huge crowds greeted them as they disembarked in the Port of New York. She'd never travelled far outside of Manchester, and had never before left the UK, but she'd made her commitment to Will and was willing to follow him to the ends of the earth, if he asked.

Once they'd disembarked from the SS Baltic and had passed fairly swiftly through customs, they had to make their way to the 42nd Street Ferry in Manhattan. This was where they would catch a ferry across the Hudson River to Weehawken, New Jersey, and where they would start their long rail journey to Chicago.

Will hailed a taxi, and they set off to 42nd Street. It would have been hard going if they'd had to carry their baggage, walking from the port to the ferry. Knowing there were occasions where they'd have to lug their bags, Will had warned Amy not to bring too many clothes and possessions with her, telling her she'd be able to buy things once they got to Chicago.

During the drive, Amy looked out at the frenetic streets. She was surprised by the number of people. Manchester was a busy city, but New York, with its bustling hordes, seemed to be populated by worker ants.

The Weehawken ferry, their vessel across the Hudson, was tiny in comparison to the ship on which they'd spent the last eight days. It was the sublime to the ridiculous.

After another trek with their luggage, and nearing the railway station, Will had suggested they stop for a meal. Amy was grateful that he knew how things worked, having done this journey before. They satisfied their appetites and then set off to buy more food for the journey; Will had warned her the food on the trains was very expensive.

Finally, replete with both nourishment and sustenance for their travels, they arrived at the West Shore Railroad. They clambered onto the Wabash Railroad's Continental Limited train, where they were going to spend the next twenty-eight hours or so travelling. The conductor directed them to their seats, and their luggage was stored safely. Amy was exhausted but forced herself to stay awake so she didn't miss anything of interest. She had already been fascinated by the strange names, Weehawken, and Wabash, and was even more so when Will surprised her by explaining that both names originated from the language of native American tribes.

The terrain that passed the train windows could have been

from a different planet, as far as Amy was concerned. Although she didn't think the scenery was as pretty as back home, she was impressed by how everything in America seemed oversized. The distances between towns, and later, states, seemed vast, so much further than she'd imagined when travelling through different 'shires' in England.

From New York, following the Hudson River, they travelled to Buffalo. As they journeyed closer, darkness crept over the landscape. Around midnight, in complete darkness, they arrived at Buffalo. Amy was disappointed as Will had told her all about the huge grain silos that loomed over the buildings around the station and she had looked forward to seeing them.

On arrival, they had to change carriages, or 'cars', as Will informed her, because the sleeper cars were to be attached to the end of the train. As they walked through the train, followed by the Pullman porter carrying their luggage, it was all a little overwhelming to Amy, and she was grateful she wasn't making the journey alone. American trains certainly were very different to those back in England.

The sleeping arrangements were quite alien too. When they reached their seats, Amy wondered where the beds were. Will explained that the upper berth was in the curved panel above their seats. She was sceptical, but she didn't have to wait long to see this transformation. Shortly afterwards, the Pullman porter returned, and using a special key-tool, lowered the upper berth. She was extremely glad to hear that Will would be sleeping in the upper berth, not only because to reach it involved clambering up a tiny ladder, but also because now she was finding it hard to keep her eyes open. Also, she didn't think it would be particularly elegant or ladylike to have to make the climb in her long skirts.

They pulled out of Buffalo and Amy fell asleep. When she woke again, Will told her he'd been awake for some time and that while they'd slept, the train had travelled along the shores of Lake Erie. The porter had been along and had locked the upper berth back into place.

As they ate the food they'd brought with them for their breakfast, Will informed her that they were coming into Detroit, and then surprised her by saying that during the night they'd travelled into Canada and back out again. She was astonished they hadn't had to stop for customs, but Will explained the two countries had open borders. Being as worn out as she'd been, she was grateful they hadn't been woken up in the night to have their passports checked!

She couldn't believe how well-informed Will was about the country. It seemed, after a day's work, he had spent most of his evenings alone, reading. She was suitably impressed by her new husband's knowledge. Every time she spoke or said the words *my husband* to herself, they brought a smile to her face. Despite being removed from all she knew back home in Manchester, here, by his side, Amy was optimistic and secure that they would make a good life together in this country.

As they left Detroit, Will said, "The next place we're going to stop in is Montpelier, Ohio, which is where the train splits. Half goes to St. Louis, and the other to Chicago."

Amy must have shown the panic she was feeling, because Will had given her an encouraging smile, as though to say, *It's perfectly easy, and we will be fine.* But from that point on, Amy started to worry. What if they were sitting in the wrong part of the train?

A couple of hours later, the train started to slow, passing the sign for Montpelier. Amy was feeling extremely nervous.

"Don't panic. We can stay on the train if you like, but we'll be sitting here for an hour at least. We may as well get off, have some lunch, and stretch our legs." Will sounded far more confident than Amy felt.

They stepped out of their sleeping car and onto the station platform, which was beginning to fill with all the other travellers from their train. Taking her arm, Will led Amy to the station hotel, which, to her relief, kept the train in view. Most of the other passengers had followed suit, and to her astonishment, considering the influx of people, the hotel staff had everything organised like clockwork. They ordered some beef stew, which arrived fairly quickly, despite the amount of people being served. Will's chatter relieved Amy of some of her tension, although she continued to surreptitiously watch what was happening to the train. For a time, she actually relaxed well enough to observe other passengers stopping to buy papers from the newsboys and other things from the hawkers selling their wares. But on hearing a whistle, she sprang up from her chair.

Will reached out and held her arm. "Amy, don't worry, that's the half of the train leaving for St. Louis."

"How do you know? Are you sure?"

"Yes. When we caught the train in Weehawken, the conductor made sure we were on the right part of the train. The company is used to this journey. They don't want to lose passengers on the way, do they?"

"I suppose you're right. I'm sorry, Will. I've just never had to undertake such a long journey as this before."

"Have a cup of tea, and when you hear the next whistle, that's when we need to get back on the train."

Amy settled back down in her chair with more composure.

Finally, she heard a whistle, and people began to make a move. Will paid for their lunch and arm in arm they walked back towards the train.

As they walked along, some youngsters rushed on ahead of their parents and ran in between everyone. Will and Amy had to unlink their arms to save themselves from being knocked over. People around them were tutting and moaning about how parents really should keep their children under control. Amy turned to see where the children had come from, and when she turned back, she couldn't see Will.

She panicked. Shouting out his name, she quickly walked a little further towards the train, but she still couldn't see him. Looking up and down the platform, she couldn't see him anywhere – there were too many people. She began to feel sick.

The conductor approached her.

"You're going to Chicago, ma'am?"

"Yes, but I seem to have lost my husband." Amy was extremely flustered compared to the porter, who didn't look at all worried.

"Don't you worry, ma'am. I'm sure he'll be here somewhere. He can't have gone far. Do you want me to help you onto the train, ma'am?"

She wasn't sure what to do. What if she got on the train and Will got left behind? But he surely wouldn't do that, because he'd done this journey before, hadn't he? Amy began to feel a little faint, when all of a sudden, strong arms moved around her shoulders, and she heard Will whisper, "Are you trying to make a run for it already, Mrs McKenzie?"

"Oh, Will, I couldn't find you." She looked up into his brown eyes, flung her arms around him, and kissed him.

The conductor coughed. "All's well then, ma'am, you've found him."

He ushered them onto the train.

Will led Amy down the car back to their seats, holding her hand. As they sat down, they heard the conductor shout, "All aboard." The train shuddered into life as they set off on the last leg of their journey to Chicago.

11

ANGLESEY, NOVEMBER 2018

As promised, Lukas turned up around the time he'd said he would arrive – at 11.30 a.m., which impressed Danny. He hadn't met him before, and although he wasn't so keen on the sports car that Lukas was driving, he seemed like a nice enough young man. Danny asked him if the car was his, and was surprised to be told "Yes", especially as it was worth more than any car he'd ever owned, and Lukas was only just twenty. He must remember to ask Jess about Lukas' family when they got back.

Jess came downstairs with her packed bag, looking radiant, which was surprising, considering how tired she'd looked at breakfast.

Lukas perched on the edge of the sofa, looking around the still unfinished room. As Jess came in, he leapt up, clearly relieved to see her.

"Have fun, you two, and please drive safely, Lukas. She's all I have." Danny kissed Jess and waved them off, remaining standing for some time after they'd gone from sight. After spending so much time together over the last year, it suddenly hit him hard. He knew over the next few years, he'd lose his little girl. It was inevitable, but he wasn't ready for that loss too.

"You okay?" Driving away with Lukas, Jess settled into the comfy leather seats of his car.

"I thought we'd stop for some lunch on the way, and have some time to ourselves before arriving at Grandfather's. If that's okay with you?"

"Sounds perfect," she replied.

Jess couldn't help feeling a little nervous about the trip as she hadn't seen Lukas in the flesh since before her mum's accident. They'd met very briefly at her funeral, but since then, she'd only spoken to him a few times on the phone. And while he'd been in Sweden, it was as if he'd disappeared off the face of the earth.

Jess glanced at him. He was incredibly handsome, not the sort of guy who she would expect to be interested in her at all. In fact, when they'd first met at Manchester Uni on her interview visit, she thought he was doing a job he'd been given by the faculty. She hadn't expected him to get in touch with her, as he had done a few weeks later. They'd planned to meet up, but she'd had to cancel due to some larger family gathering she'd been told she couldn't miss, and then, by the time they got in contact again, the accident had happened, and her whole life had changed. She'd been very touched to see him at the funeral. She knew most other young guys would run a mile from something like that.

Lukas was glancing over at her. "You look sad."

"Sorry. No, I'm fine. I was just thinking about when we met, and how it's taken so long for us to get real time together." She smiled at him as if to prove she was fine. "So, what's your grandad like? Is he a very stern Scandinavian?"

Lukas laughed. "He can be stern, I'll give you that, but Scandinavian—I don't think he's ever been to Sweden in his life. He's got a nondescript accent, so it's hard to tell where he's from. And he's definitely 'Grandfather', not 'Grandad'."

"Okay, 'Grandfather' it is. Seriously? I can't believe he's not been to Sweden. If I had family there, I'd be visiting all the time." She hadn't meant it to sound as though she was angling for an invitation. She quickly changed the focus. "Tell me about your trip. Was it your first visit, or have you been lots of times before?"

"I have been before, but a long while ago, when I was little, and I didn't really remember much. But, I think I told you when I rang, this time, we went to visit Vaxholm where my great-grandfather was born. We didn't meet any relatives there, though there must be some out there somewhere."

Lukas chatted about the rest of his trip as they drove along the main road that led across from mainland Wales into Anglesey.

Finally, they stopped at the place he was taking her for lunch. Even in winter, it was a beautiful spot, and the restaurant had views out across the sea and the beach that stretched around the bay.

"We can go for a walk afterwards – if you've brought warm enough clothes. It's going to be pretty windy down there," Lukas said.

"I've got my woolly hat and some gloves. I'll be warm enough. I can't wait to get down there. That sandy beach looks amazing. Ours is too pebbly."

"At least it's a beach. All I have is the metropolis that is Manchester."

"And bright lights and city life," Jess cut in. "I can't wait to get to somewhere livelier than Llaneirw. It's too quiet."

They chatted easily over their meal, and afterwards, Lukas took her hand as they walked along the beach. Jess could feel her head clearing as the brisk wind tried to creep below her hat, which was pulled down low to keep her warm. They walked for about an hour, stopping to pick up pebbles, clamber over rocks, gaze out to sea – all the time both seeming to recognise the comfort of each other's company.

Back on the road, their journey was shorter than Jess had imagined. After only another twenty minutes or so, they arrived at the town of Amlwch.

"Grandfather's house is only a short way from here. It's a little isolated, but the old boy has a couple who look out for him, Delyth and Konrad Brunner. They live in a small cottage next to his house. Delyth does his cooking, cleaning, and welcomes visitors, and her husband looks after the grounds and does any maintenance required. They've been with him for years."

"How old is your grandfather?"

"A grumpy seventy-four, I think. He doesn't like being retired, and still wants to control everything about the company, much to my dad's annoyance."

"What about your grandmother?"

"She died in 2005. She had breast cancer."

Lukas went silent for a moment. Jess was concentrating on his driving but saw he was obviously upset.

"I'm sorry, I didn't mean to pry."

"No, it's fine. I loved Mormor Helena. She was a wonderful lady. I never know how she ended up with someone like my grandfather."

"What do you mean? You're not selling him well. If I'm going to be spending some time under his roof, I hope he's not as grumpy as you make him out to be." Jess laughed. "Why 'Mormor', by the way?"

"It's the Swedish name for 'grandmother'."

"So, was she Swedish? I thought you said your grandfather hadn't been to Sweden?"

"No, she wasn't, but my mum is Swedish, and she referred to

Helena as Mormor, so it stuck." Lukas changed down gears as he slowed down. "Well, you'll be able to judge for yourself. We're here." A small sign on one of the two brick pillars either side of a turning declared: Tŷ Glasfryn.

"What does 'Tŷ Glasfryn' mean?" Jess asked.

Lukas gave her a quick glance and shrugged his shoulders. "D' you know, I've not got an idea," Lukas answered as he turned off between the pillars, down the muddy track which eventually opened out onto a concrete drive. He parked in front of an impressive, though odd-looking, old house surrounded by wispy trees.

Jess got out of the car and looked around. As Lukas had said, it appeared to be isolated, even though it wasn't that far from the town. Other than the house, outbuildings and the small cottage, where she assumed the Brunners lived, the house stood surrounded by trees which blocked any views there may have been. She had hoped to see the sea. Over the last few months, Jess had got used to being able to see and hear the sea each day. She hadn't realised how much it comforted her. Even though Llaneirw wasn't the hive of activity, the sound of the sea was like a consoling hug. Here, not being able to see any other signs of life felt oppressive.

"Come on, let's get in and meet the old boy." Lukas, carrying their bags, led the way to the front door. Before he could knock, the door opened, revealing a smiling middle-aged lady, who introduced herself to Jess as Delyth. Her lovely, gently lilting Welsh accent welcomed them. She hugged Lukas and then smiled at Jess. Happily chatting away, she led them into the warmth of the house.

Jess spent her time looking around. She was fascinated by the place. On the outside, although it looked impressive, it was old-fashioned, with its sash windows and the canopied veranda along its front. However, internally, someone had decorated the house fairly recently. Although some of what she assumed to be original features of the old house remained, the inside was more welcoming than the exterior. Jess hoped that Lukas' grandfather would be the same. She had to wait to find out because Delyth led them upstairs to their rooms, informing them on the way that Sir Robert was on the phone at present but would join them in the lounge in half an hour.

"This is your room, miss. You have your own en suite, so you should have everything you need." Delyth opened the door to a large bedroom, which was fairly sparse, apart from the bed, a wardrobe and a chest of drawers, and the door into the en suite. It seemed the room wasn't used regularly, and the only decoration was a large painting over the bed and a small vase of fresh flowers on the chest of drawers.

"Thank you, Delyth."

"I'll come and fetch you in a mo," Lukas said as he followed Delyth to the other end of the house.

By the time Lukas knocked on her door, Jess had unpacked, freshened herself up, put on a smarter top and was looking out of the window.

"Is your room okay?"

"Yeah, it's great, thanks. My own en suite is handy."

"You realise my crafty grandfather has put you in a room opposite his. He obviously wants to stop any 'hanky-panky', as he calls it."

Jess laughed nervously, not sure what to say. She certainly fancied Lukas, and they got on brilliantly, but she hadn't honestly been expecting them to leap on each other while under his grandfather's roof.

Lukas seemed to notice Jess' awkwardness and said, "Sorry, he is just so transparent. When I've visited with mates, he's put us both in the rooms next to each other so we don't disturb him. I found it funny. I didn't mean to embarrass you."

"It's fine, don't worry." Jess changed the subject. "Can you see the sea from your room?"

"Come and have a look." Lukas seemed happy to change the subject too. He walked ahead of her down the corridor and Jess noticed the creaking floorboards, which she hadn't even heard when they first came upstairs. She smiled to herself. The old boy really was crafty.

Lukas' room was far more personalised. On top of his chest of drawers were photos of him and his mates, some with people she presumed were his family, and his stuff was scattered around the room. He had some sailing gear stacked in one corner, and a pile of books by the bed. He grabbed her hand and took her over to the window. "If you look over there to the left, you can just about see the sea in the distance, well normally. It's got a bit cloudy now, so it's harder to see, but on a good day, you can just pick out the blue of the sea on the horizon."

When Jess turned around, Lukas was much closer than she'd realised. He gave her a quick kiss on her mouth, smiled, and moved away into the room. It wasn't a romantic kiss, just a light touch, so quick she hadn't been able to respond by kissing him back, but even so, it sent shivers through her body.

As though nothing had happened, Lukas said, "You ready to go down and meet Grandfather?"

"Yeah. Do I look smart enough for him?"

"You look beautiful as ever. Anyway, he's not the style police, so don't worry."

Jess laughed. Lukas took her hand and led her downstairs to meet Sir Robert.

Lukas' grandfather was reading a book when they entered the lounge. A roaring, open fire warmed the large room. Sir Robert stood up and extended his hand to Jess. "Pleased to meet you, young lady. It's a nice change for Lukas to bring someone other than his loud mates to visit me. I'm looking forward to a more sedate visit this time." He turned and grabbed Lukas, pulling him into his body and giving him a bear hug.

Lukas laughed and returned the hug. "I don't know what makes you think she's going to be quieter than my mates. Not all girls are so refined these days, you know." He pulled a face at Jess and then looked back at his grandfather. "Haven't you ever heard of 'ladettes'?" Winking at Jess, he continued. "Though I will say, Jess is not one."

"Thanks, Lukas, you had me worried there."

"Come and tell me about yourself while we wait for Delyth to call us in for dinner," Sir Robert said.

Jess started to explain about her move from Liverpool, although she left out the reason for moving. She told him where she'd met Lukas, and that she would be going to Manchester University next term. Luckily, Delyth came in to announce that dinner was ready, so she didn't have to put up with any more 'vetting'.

Although Jess was still feeling full from lunch, Delyth's cooking was something to savour. She was a fantastic cook, so Jess wasn't surprised that Sir Robert had quite a broad girth.

After their meal, they returned to the lounge, where Delyth would bring them coffee.

"Lukas, where are you going to take young Jess tomorrow?" his grandfather asked.

"Jess asked me if I'd take her over the Cemaes Bay. I will if the weather isn't too bad. There's not much to do there otherwise, though it's a good drive."

"Why are you interested in going there, Jess?"

She hadn't even told Lukas yet, so she definitely wasn't going to tell his grandfather the real reason.

"I found something in the local library about a woman

whose husband went down on the *Aliciana,* and it said that a lot of the survivors, and the victims' bodies, were taken there."

"That's a bit morbid for a pretty young thing like you, isn't it?" Sir Robert asked.

"I don't see why," Lukas said. "It's all history, and it will be interesting to see if they have anything about the ship."

Sir Robert looked as though they'd said something that caused him some discomfort and he made a quiet 'harumph' sound. Jess met Lukas' eyes, then both quickly had to look away to stop themselves from laughing.

"Pub?" Lukas asked, smiling at Jess.

Sir Robert said, "Well, I'll see you both in the morning then. I'll be in bed by the time you two get back. Don't make too much noise."

Lukas had suggested a visit to The Griffin's Arms, a pub in Amlwch that he and his mates usually frequented when they visited his grandfather. It was a busy pub and a good size, with some cosy corners that looked appealing for quieter conversations. After getting them both drinks, Lukas led the way to two comfy chairs in an alcove not far from the large, blazing fire. Jess was more relaxed than she'd been for months. Lukas put her at her ease, and even when his grandfather had questioned her about wanting to visit Cemaes, he had come to her defence.

"So, are you going to tell me why you really want to go to Cemaes? I didn't realise you were a history buff."

Jess took a deep breath, deciding she wasn't quite ready to tell him everything. "I'm not, but Dad and me have found out that a lady who lived in our house, Amy, was on the *Aliciana,* and she survived, but her husband went down with the ship."

"Shit, that's harsh."

Jess nodded.

"Were they an old couple, or what?" Lukas asked.

"No. They'd only married a year or two before, and they were on their way home from Chicago when the ship went down."

"When was this?"

"1915, during the First World War. But the worst thing is, his wife lived until 1958. That was forty-three years alone. Can you imagine?"

Lukas looked very thoughtful. "You know I think my great-grandfather was on that ship."

"Seriously?"

"Well, Grandfather is always going on about his dad, the 'hero'. He's very proud of him, but I haven't always listened, to be honest. When I was younger, I didn't see much of him. He and my dad don't get on that well, and after Mormor died, we stopped visiting altogether. I've only started visiting the last few years. I do remember, though, when Grandfather talked about his dad, I just got used to accepting that he saw him as this big hero. As stupid as it sounds, I've never really looked into why."

"Well, maybe you should ask him?" Jess couldn't believe that Lukas' family was also linked to the ship. This was just too weird.

"We'll ask him to tell us about his dad tomorrow, if he's around. He often goes off golfing, or meeting up with business mates, when I come to stay. I don't always see much of him. He's never been that interested in us grandchildren. Mind you, he's always been good at gifts."

"Perhaps that's his way of making up for not being interested," Jess ventured.

"Yeah, maybe."

Lukas went off to order another drink. Jess tried to decide if she should tell him how she knew about Amy.

Lukas had obviously been thinking about things too. As he sat down with the drinks, he asked, "What did you say the woman who lived in your house was called?"

"Amy."

"Yeah. Do you know what Amy looked like?"

Jess pulled the locket from under the neck of her sweater and leant forward to show Lukas the picture of Amy inside.

"Wow! Where did you get that?"

"As you may have noticed"—she stopped to laugh—"Dad is renovating the house. He pulled up the floorboards in my room because I could see there was something shiny in there, and this is what we found." She couldn't believe how easily she'd lied. As relaxed as she was with Lukas, she didn't want to scare him off with the truth. She enjoyed his company, and he seemed to like hers too. She changed the subject. "Come on, I still want to hear more about Sweden. Tell me all about it. Everything. Where you stayed, what the weather was like, what you ate. All of it."

Lukas did just that. He gave her a long description about the entire holiday. By the end, she almost felt like she'd been there with him. "I'll have to take you sometime," he said.

Jess was lost in the moment. She leant forward and kissed him. "Sorry. I was so excited about that. I didn't mean to..."

Lukas smiled and grabbed the hand that wasn't holding her glass. "It's fine, I'm glad you did. Now I don't feel so bad doing this." He leant in and gave her a long, gentle kiss.

Like earlier, when he'd kissed her lightly, her whole body quivered, only this time, the feeling went much deeper. Jess pulled apart and looked around. Not that she was shy about being seen kissing, but she wasn't really one for public displays of affection – 'PDAs', as she and her friends called them. Maybe he was interested in her as more than a friend.

The drive back to Tŷ Glasfryn was in silence, although for most of the drive, Lukas held her hand. Back at the house, Lukas leant over and kissed her, and yet again, she could feel her body melt at his touch. He pulled away quite abruptly and got out of the car. Jess followed him into the house. Taking her hand, he pulled her up the stairs, stopping at the top to give her a very quick, light kiss. "I need to cool down. I'll see you in the morning."

Once she was alone in her room, she texted Fran to update her on the Lukas front, half floating on air and half feeling incredibly frustrated.

Next morning, Lukas knocked on her door to walk down to breakfast with her, where they were greeted by Sir Robert, who was busy reading the newspaper, loudly crunching his way through his bowl of cereal. "Morning" was the only greeting they got from him. Eventually, he put the paper down and smiled at them both. "So, what are you doing today? Off to Cemaes? The weather looks pretty good, so it might be worth going today."

"Probably, yes. Erm, Grandfather, I'm sure you probably have told me this before, but was your dad on the *Aliciana*?"

Sir Robert looked a little flushed. "Yes, he was. He was a survivor." He took a sip of his tea. "He was hailed as a hero because he helped so many people get to safety in the lifeboats." He beamed with pride as he mentioned this.

"You've got some pictures you can show Jess, haven't you? She might find them interesting, especially if there are any of the actual ship."

"I'll look some out for later, before dinner." He suddenly stood up and disappeared out of the room.

"Something I said?" Lukas looked at Jess and laughed. "Well, you might actually get to see some photos. I think he's got one on the wall in his study. I can vaguely remember it from when I was younger, but I've not been in there for years."

"So, is the weather good enough to visit Cemaes today?" Jess asked, feeling a little apprehensive about later, with no idea why.

"Yep. Make sure you've got lots of warm clothes because it can be incredibly windy this time of the year. It's a great shame that it isn't better weather– we could have gone sailing too. Maybe another time."

The drive to Cemaes was again far shorter than Jess had imagined, but as Lukas had mentioned, it was a beautiful drive, if very breezy. The land on either side of the road seemed to be mostly farmland. They even passed some wind turbines in one field – probably the perfect place for them. By the way some trees and bushes leant, it was possible to see just how stormy it got. In places it looked as though the prevailing winds had almost made the trees bend low in homage to the earth from which they'd sprung. Just after passing the sign for Cemaes, the sea appeared on the horizon, glittering in the winter sun.

After parking the car and donning her woolly hat and gloves, Jess followed Lukas down to the water's edge. It was extremely windy, and the cold tried to seep in between her layers of clothing. Looking out into the breadth of the Irish Sea, she was suddenly filled with deep anguish and grief, and before she could stop herself, her eyes filled with tears, and she started crying. From what she'd read, Amy had never been to Cemaes, and when the memorial services were held, she was still recovering in Manchester with Will's relatives. Yet it was her sensibilities that were invading Jess' emotions. Hoping Lukas hadn't noticed, she tried to wipe away the tears, but of course, he had. He looked at her with great care and pulled him towards her, hugging her close.

Eventually able to control her sobs, she said, "Sorry, I couldn't help it. I suddenly felt a wave of utter grief."

"Don't be sorry. You don't have to explain. I'm sure your mum's death hits you when you least expect it."

Jess looked up into his beautiful blue, reassuring eyes, feeling slightly guilty yet weirdly relieved that he assumed her tears were for her mum. She knew this grief was Amy's, not her own. This was near where the *Aliciana* went down and where she lost the love of her life; out there in the Irish Sea. Jess couldn't explain that to Lukas, not yet.

They walked around the bay for a while before going to a café for a warm drink. Afterwards, they went to find the little church where some of the victims had been interred, and where a small memorial stood, in remembrance of those who drowned on the *Aliciana*. There was a lot of information Jess hadn't seen before. A lighthouse keeper on The Skerries had seen the *Aliciana* listing and had raised the alarm. Jess could feel Amy's turmoil deep inside herself. She was walking and talking, but Amy was guiding her where to look and what to read. As she stood looking across the churchyard out to sea, she began to shiver, and Lukas put his arm around her, which brought her back to the present.

"Come on, I think it's time to get back home and into the warmth, don't you?"

Jess smiled up at him, grateful for his gentle manner. Most of the guys she'd been out with seemed totally unaware of her feelings. She wasn't used to such empathy from someone only a few years older than herself.

When they'd arrived back at the house, Jess had told Lukas she was going to have a rest for a while. Lukas had said he was going to take the time to catch up with his grandfather so he could give his dad an update when he went home.

A knocking sound woke Jess abruptly from her sleep. It took her a while to remember where she was. Lukas' voice from the other side of the door asked, "Are you ready for dinner?"

"Oh, okay, I'll be with you in about ten minutes." For no

reason that she could imagine, Jess was feeling nervous because she knew Sir Robert was going to show her photos of his father. She splashed water over her face, changed her jumper, and after tidying her hair, went downstairs.

Dinner was a fairly quiet affair. Sir Robert didn't seem much in the mood for conversation, and even when Lukas asked him a question, he seemed distant.

When they'd finished another wonderful home-cooked meal prepared by Delyth, Lukas reminded his grandfather about them looking at the photos. They followed him into his study, which was exactly what Jess would have imagined it to look like. Dark-brown furniture, with brown leather chairs and two of the walls entirely lined with bookshelves. The leather chairs stood either side of an open fire, which added some warmth to the room. Sir Robert pointed up at the framed photo hanging above the fireplace. "That's my father, Peter."

Jess looked at the image and had a feeling of déjà vu. She couldn't think where she'd seen him before, but he looked familiar. *It must be family likeness,* she thought. She moved a little closer and gazed at the photo. As she looked, the pain she'd previously felt returned to her side. She stood back from the photo and looked at Lukas. Feeling as though she was going to pass out, she quickly sat down in one of the large leather chairs and held onto her side.

Lukas was immediately beside her. "Are you okay? Do you need a drink?"

Jess nodded, uncertain whether she could speak. Lukas rushed off and then reappeared with a glass of water, which she sipped slowly. All the while, Sir Robert just stared into the distance.

When she was able to speak again, she said, "I'm sorry, I don't know what happened. I suddenly had a pain in my side."

"Perhaps something you ate?" asked Lukas.

“Maybe, but I doubt it. Delyth’s cooking is excellent. Sorry to be such a pain.”

Sir Robert, sitting in the chair opposite, now looked perplexed. He clearly wasn’t used to dealing with young women. It seemed to Jess that he had no idea what to say or do and was glad his grandson had taken control.

“I think I’d better go to bed early, Lukas. Maybe I got a chill today, I don’t know...”

“That’s a good idea. You’ll probably feel fine tomorrow. I’ll help you upstairs, just in case.”

Lukas got Jess to her feet. She was unable to stand up straight and still clutched her side. They left Sir Robert sitting by the fire.

“Are you sure you’ll be okay?” Lukas said on the way up to Jess’ room. “Do you want me to get Delyth to fill a hot water bottle for you?”

“No, I’ll be okay, I’m sure. Thank you. I’m sorry for being such a pain.”

Lukas kissed her on her forehead and went back downstairs, leaving Jess sitting on her bed. As soon as he’d gone, she carefully stood up and went to the mirror. Lifting her jumper, she was shocked to see the large, dark bruise had reappeared on her side. It was exactly where the bruise had appeared when she’d dreamt about Will being attacked on the ship. She began running her fingers around the edge of the gold locket.

12

The next morning, after a restless night, Jess' side was less painful. Looking in the mirror, she saw the bruising had lessened too. However, her head was buzzing with thoughts. Why did Lukas' great-grandfather look familiar to her? It didn't make any sense. She decided she wouldn't dwell on it, not while she was here with Lukas. She didn't want him to think she was a feeble girl who spent her time crying and being ill. It was their third day away, so today, she would prove to him that she was just as capable as anyone else.

Over breakfast, she suggested perhaps they could go for a coastal walk, saying the windy weather would blow away any chills or stuff going on in her head. If they walked from Amlwch, as long as they didn't go anywhere near Cemaes, Jess hoped Amy would stay out of her head.

Lukas decided they'd drive to Amlwch, and then see how far they could walk on the coastal path. He said it wouldn't be so easy to walk at this time of year because of the mud and slippery rocks, but they could take a look.

To be honest, although the sky was blue, it was very cold and the wind was quite brutal. Jess was beginning to worry if she could live up to her ideal of being capable. But Lukas seemed to be finding it as hard going as she was, so she didn't feel so bad. After they'd walked for about three quarters of an hour, he decided they should give up, and they walked back to town. She had to admit, though, the views would be stunning in sunnier weather.

Back in town, they went to The Griffin's Arms again and had lunch. Despite both knowing that later they would have a filling dinner cooked by Delyth, they thought they deserved food to make up for the strenuous battle against the wind. Well, that's what they managed to persuade each other.

"You're much brighter today," Lukas said.

"Yes. I don't know what happened yesterday." Jess looked at Lukas, trying to decide whether to say anything about his great-grandfather. "It was odd...I don't know why, but your great-grandfather looked familiar." She continued before he could say anything. "I know there is a family likeness, but it was something more. As stupid as this sounds, it was as though I'd met him." To her relief, Lukas didn't look at her as though she was a nutter, although he did look intrigued.

"Well, that would be difficult, unless you're reincarnated and living your second life, because he died way before either of us were born. It must be the family likeness."

Jess nodded. But she couldn't let go of the feeling that she'd heard him speaking, the memory of which made her uncomfortable. She changed the subject and started talking about Manchester, saying she was looking forward to going to university next year. Lukas told her about the places he'd introduce her to, which pleased her because he seemed to be assuming they'd meet up when she was there.

After lunch, Jess asked him where she could buy a present for her dad and Fran, so he took her off to a gift shop on the

High Street. While they were in the shop, he had a phone call and went outside to answer it. When he returned, he wasn't smiling.

"What's up?" Jess asked.

"That was Grandfather. He says he's got to go to Liverpool for a couple of days, and he wants to give Delyth and Konrad some time off, so do we mind leaving tomorrow morning? Talk about making us feel welcome."

For the first time, Jess saw Lukas look annoyed.

"That's not a problem. I've enjoyed visiting and seeing Cemaes and here. Don't worry."

Back at the house, Jess decided to have a soak in the bath and then pack her stuff; she didn't want to waste time in the morning. At dinner, Lukas was still angry with his grandfather, so the atmosphere was odd, although Jess didn't understand why Lukas was so irritated. They were Sir Robert's guests, so it was up to him when they left.

Before she left, though, Jess wanted to take another look at the photo in Sir Robert's study. But she didn't want him in there too. She wondered if she could sneak in at some point but didn't want to appear rude. In the end, she told Lukas she wanted to see the photo again, asking if she could go in when his grandfather wasn't in there. If he thought it an odd request, he didn't say so, and he suggested she went in after dinner, saying he would keep his grandfather busy.

As planned, after dinner, Jess crept into the study, shutting the door quietly behind her. She put the light on and went up to the photo. Like the day before, she had a sinking feeling in the pit of her stomach. This man had done something horrible. She knew him. She had seen him, but it was like when you can't remember a word – it's in your mind somewhere, but just out of reach. She just couldn't grasp hold of how and why she recognised him.

Jess quietly left the study and rejoined Lukas and his grandfather.

"I won't see you in the morning, so I want to say goodbye now. It's been good to meet you, Jess." Sir Robert held out his hand to shake hers.

Jess thanked him in return, said goodnight to Lukas, and went up to bed.

She slept deeply and soundly, grateful not to be kept awake with dreams or worrying about things she couldn't quite get her head around.

The drive home went smoothly, and well before lunchtime, they arrived back in Llaneirw. Danny was surprised to see them back so quickly but was secretly pleased to see Jess. He'd missed her more than he'd expected.

"Did you have a good time?" he asked as soon as they got through the door. "The house was too quiet without you."

"Yeah, it was good. Lukas' grandfather has an interesting house, and we took some trips out." She smiled at Lukas, who was still standing in the doorway. "Come in, Lukas, don't stand there. Do you want to stay for some lunch before you drive back?"

Lukas looked surprised. "Yes. Please. I'm not in a rush to get back to Manchester, you know."

"Oh, I thought you'd probably have things on," Jess said. "Er, if you want, you could stay here tonight." Her voice trailed off.

Lukas' face lit up. "That'd be great. Do you mind, Mr Graham?" he asked Danny.

"Not at all, Lukas. And, call me Danny. Mr Graham is my dad!"

Danny held back his excitement to show Jess the almost finished kitchen and lounge. So, rather than interrupt what he recognised as a slight awkwardness between Lukas and Jess, he suggested they all go to The Blue Dolphin and he'd treat them to lunch. "Just dump your bags here. We can sort them when we get back." He grabbed his jacket and led the way to the pub.

After a chatty lunch, the three of them wandered back to the house, and Danny chose this as the time to show Jess the kitchen. She was suitably impressed with what he'd done.

"I love it. I love the layout and the colour. What are you going to have on the floor?" she asked while opening doors and running her hands over the newly finished worktops.

"What about wood? I could continue it into the lounge. We can pick it out together as you have such a good eye for colour."

"Thanks, Dad. The lounge looks good too." Jess hugged him.

"What do you think, Lukas?"

"I'm impressed. My dad couldn't do anything like this. He'd just pay someone else to do it. It looks so much better than before we left. In fact, pretty amazing. Did you get any sleep while we've been away?"

Danny smiled. "I have to admit, I did get some help from the plumber. A nice guy my neighbour recommended, and we got on well, so when he offered to help out with some bits, I was more than happy to accept. He did me a great deal too."

"Well, either way, you've done a great job, Dad." Jess hugged him again. "So, you're not rushing off, are you, Lukas? You're staying over and setting off in the morning?"

"I don't want to put you out when you've got all of this going on." He looked from Jess to Danny.

Danny said, "Go on, stay, then you can have a drink and catch up for a little longer before you go."

"We've got a spare room. It's not The Ritz or anything, but there's a bed, and it's quite comfy. You just have to share the room with a few boxes here and there."

Jess led Lukas up the stairs to show him where to put his stuff. Passing her room, she told him to come and find her when he'd sorted out his bags.

A few minutes later, Lukas knocked on her door.

"Wow, love the colours," Lukas said, looking around, first at her pictures, then he turned to look out at the view. "It's not a bad space."

Jess put on one of her favourite playlists and sat on the bed watching him. He came over and sat next to her. Without warning, he leant over and started kissing her. Not just a peck, but a long, sensuous kiss that lingered, seeming to last forever.

Coming up for air, Lukas said, "I've been wanting to do that all week."

Jess smiled and pulled him back towards her, saying, "So have I."

Gently, he pushed her back onto the bed, continuing to kiss her, his hands caressing her body. She groaned, lost in the moment. Her body ached with desire. Jess wanted him so badly, but not here, at home, with her dad downstairs.

Both were breathing heavily, and eventually, she pulled away, saying, "I'm sorry, Lukas. I can't, not here. But I do want you. Just not with my dad in the house."

"No, I'm sorry, I couldn't control what's been pent up inside me all week." He gave her a quick kiss, then moving away from her a little more, straightened his clothes. "There'll be plenty of time in the future."

Jess stood up, walked over to him, and kissed him. "I wish there was somewhere we could go. I want you too." She exhaled slowly. "Come on, let's go for a walk down by the sea. The wind will cool us down."

Jess grabbed Lukas' hands and pulled him towards the door, straightening her clothes on the way and leading him downstairs.

"We're just going out for a walk, Dad," she yelled as they walked out of the door.

Later that night, lying in bed, Jess found it hard to sleep, knowing that Lukas was in the spare room down the corridor. It was incredibly hard to stop herself from creeping into his room and bed, but there was no way that she was going to have sex while her dad was in hearing of her. Finally, overly tired, she fell asleep.

She knew she was on a ship, feeling the engine's movement under her feet, and the room where she stood was filled with machines. Jess recognised by the dials and the sounds of crackling radio waves in the background that it was a radio room. The man in front of her was wearing uniform, including a cap with the logo of an 'M' on the front. His dark eyes were menacing and cold. He leant closer to her face and said words she'd heard before.

"You shouldn't stick your nose into other people's business, Mr McKenzie."

Instantly, the agonising, sharp pain in her side appeared yet again, and to her horror, for the first time, she comprehended the fact. The man was pushing a knife deeper into her body, twisting it as it went. The pain was the most terrible thing she'd ever felt in her life. She collapsed as the man pushed her away from him.

At that exact moment, she woke, screaming in agony, holding on to her side. The excruciating pain was stopping her from breathing. By the noise she was making, she was surprised she hadn't woken the whole street. Still unable to catch her breath, she tried to sit up, but it was far too painful. Danny came running into her room, followed by a dazed Lukas.

"Another bad dream?" Danny asked.

The pain was so bad Jess still couldn't answer. She just nodded.

"Can you grab a glass of water, please, Lukas?" Danny directed him to the bathroom. He looked back at Jess, who was still having problems. "Try to take deep breaths, love."

Slowly and painfully, Jess managed to calm down her breathing, until she was able to speak.

"I'm so sorry, I didn't mean to wake you both. I had a terrible dream."

Lukas looked dumbstruck; he obviously hadn't ever seen or heard anyone wake from such a bad dream. "Are you sure you're okay?"

"Yes, I'm fine. Go back to sleep. I'll see you in the morning. I'm fine, honestly." Jess gave him a feeble smile.

"If you really are sure you're okay?" He hovered for a few seconds, still uncertain.

"Yeah, anyway, Dad's with me, so go back to bed. I'll see you in the morning."

With a look of worry on his face, Lukas left the room. Danny remained sitting on her bed, his arm around her. "You didn't have any dreams while you were away, did you?"

"No, but I didn't expect to. I'll explain everything to you tomorrow after Lukas has left. Okay?"

Danny nodded. He sat with her for a while, stroking her hair. Only after Jess shooed him away did he go back to his own room, although Jess remained sitting up.

She looked around the room. Speaking quietly, she said, "Amy, are you there?"

From the room's darkest corner, Amy appeared.

"Amy, I know how Will died. He was murdered because of something he saw. I don't know what he saw, but I do know who killed him."

Inside her head, she heard Amy's cry of anguish and her question. *Who?*

"My friend's great-grandfather." Jess realised she was crying silently. She wasn't certain if they were her own tears or those of Amy.

How do you know? Amy's voice asked.

"I saw his photograph when I visited Lukas' grandfather and felt sick as soon as I saw him, but then, didn't know why. Now I do. I saw him kill your husband. I'm so sorry, Amy."

A cool waft of air moved across her shoulders and she knew Amy was closer.

"I promise you I'm going to do all I can to find out why Will was murdered."

Again, she heard Amy's voice thank her, feeling another waft of cool air across her hair and down onto her face – reminding her of how her mum often used to grasp the side of her head, cupping her cheeks before kissing her. Jess wondered if Amy had done the same thing or if she had imagined it.

Part of Jess was relieved because now she knew exactly who killed Will. But how on earth was she going to prove it? How could she explain to anyone now that the ghost of a dead man had shown her how he was killed?

Carefully, she slid down the bed, holding her side so as not to reawaken the pain that was still there.

Sometime later, Jess was asleep, and Amy stood at the end of her bed, keeping guard. This young girl had found some truth for her. Now she knew why Will was unable to rest. His death needed avenging. She needed to know what he'd seen that was so important he needed to be killed.

13

Jess dreaded seeing Lukas at breakfast. What was she going to say to him about waking everyone up last night? She pulled on her jumper, gave her hair a quick shake, and walked downstairs. Danny was already eating, with Lukas seated opposite at the new kitchen island, drinking coffee. They both looked up as Jess entered the room.

"Good morning. Are you feeling better?" Danny asked.

"Yeah, much better, thanks. Morning, Lukas." Jess smiled at him quickly, then distracted herself by pouring some coffee and tipping far too much cereal into a bowl.

After a short while, Lukas asked the question. The elephant in the room.

"So, do you often have such terrible dreams? I heard your dad say, 'Another bad dream'."

Jess looked at Danny, who was about to answer, and shot him a look to say, *Keep quiet.*

"Sometimes, yeah, but not all the time, I'm glad to say. Sorry I woke you too."

"That wasn't why I mentioned it. I was worried about it. You looked so terrified. So scared," Lukas said. "I don't want to pry, but—"

"Then don't." Jess answered, more curtly than she'd meant to.

Lukas looked hurt and continued to drink his coffee. Jess returned to work her way through the mountain of cereal she'd given herself.

Danny stood up and put his coffee mug in the dishwasher. "I've got some work to do upstairs. See you before you go, Lukas. And thanks for taking Jess away this week."

"No problem. Thanks, Danny."

Danny made a hasty retreat.

"Can't you tell me about the dreams, Jess? I only want to know because I care about you. You must know that, don't you?" Lukas said.

Jess was torn. She still didn't want to tell him about Amy, because she knew it made her appear mad. Yet at the same time, she didn't want to push him away. "Okay, but you need to let me explain before you say anything." She looked at him for his agreement. Lukas nodded. "I sometimes have dreams that seem to be linked to real life. Dreams about things that have actually happened. Last night, I dreamt about your great-grandfather killing someone who was on the *Aliciana*. But when I dream, it's as though I'm one of the people in the dream, and last night I was the person he killed." She hadn't been looking at his face while she'd spoken, but now looked up at him.

Lukas looked dumbstruck. "I'm sorry, but that sounds ludicrous. How am I supposed to believe you?"

Jess continued. "I'll show you. Sometimes, I even get physical bruises. Look." And she pulled up her jumper to show Lukas the dark bruise on her side. He reached out and touched it, and she winced.

"That looks terrible, but it can't be real. You can't be hurt in a dream." He looked again at the terrible, dark bruise on Jess' side. "Are you sure you didn't do that before you went to sleep, and forgot?"

"Do you really think I'm that stupid and clumsy? No, of course I'd remember if I did something like that when I was awake." Jess glared at Lukas. "Do you remember how I reacted to the photo of your great-grandfather? Well, I knew I had seen him."

"But you can't have, can you, Jess? I know my own grandfather is harsh sometimes, but I can't believe my great-grandfather was a murderer."

"Neither could I, knowing you, but—"

Jess recoiled as Lukas raised his voice in desperation, interrupting her.

"Are you seriously trying to tell me that you believe your dreams are true?"

Without even considering her answer, she replied. "Yes."

Lukas stood up and paced backwards and forwards. "Jess, listen to yourself. You can't know beyond proof that just because you had a weird reaction to my great-grandfather's photo, and then saw him in a dream killing someone, that it's true. That's... tha...that's just madness, and I know you're not mad! Maybe it's something psychosomatic. Are you sure it's not something that is being caused by your grief?"

Jess was hurt and angry. "No, it's not. Don't bring my mum into this. It's nothing to do with her."

"I'm sorry, Jess, but I can't think of a logical reason."

Jess glared at him. "I know what I dreamt. Next time you see your grandfather, ask him if his father wore a cap with an 'M' logo on it when he was on the *Aliciana*."

Lukas looked at her as though she were a stranger. His look froze her heart, and she knew, in that moment, she'd lost him.

"I'm not going to ask him anything. This is stupid, Jess. I'm sorry, but I'm going home. Maybe I'll ring you when I get there."

He walked out of the house, slamming the door behind him.

Danny came rushing down the stairs. He found Jess sobbing. "Oh, love, I'm sorry." Danny held her until her crying subsided.

Pulling up her jumper, she showed Danny the bruise. "He didn't even believe this. He thinks it must be psychosomatic. Dad, he thinks I'm mad."

He pulled her towards him again. "Look, this has got to stop! It isn't doing you any good. I'm going to call Sally and get her to do that spiritual cleaning thingy she does."

Despite everything, he actually made Jess laugh.

"It's a spiritual cleanse, not like spring cleaning! No, I set out to help Amy, and I'm going to finish. The bruise will wear off in a day or two, and at least I've been able to tell Amy what happened to Will. I'm not stopping now. Now I need to do some more research into what the 'M' means on his cap, and find out a bit more about the *Aliciana* crew. Fran will help, and if we don't know where to look, she says her sister Kyra will help us. She's a journalist."

"Are you sure, love? I can't bear seeing you hurt or so upset."

"Yes." With more conviction than she believed, she continued. "I'm sure Lukas will ring later when he's calmed down. I'm sure it'll be okay."

But Lukas didn't call the next day or the next. He didn't call before Christmas, either, and in the end, Jess told herself that it was over. She had pushed him away by telling him the truth. And her dad was pussy-footing around her too. She knew he was being careful not to mention Anglesey or Lukas.

Christmas was a time they'd both been dreading. As it was only the two of them, it was quiet, but they both tried hard to make it as normal as they could. They didn't have a tree, because that had been a big tradition when Kate was alive. The three of them would decorate the tree the weekend before Christmas Day, drink too much wine, and generally have a laugh. A tree would have been too much for them this year; just one more thing reminding them she wasn't there. Instead, Danny and Jess bought a few decorations that they put around the room, including lots of candles, which they lit each night, their warm glow adding a comfy atmosphere to the room.

On Christmas Eve, Jess had arranged to meet Fran in the pub for a drink, and rather than leave her dad home alone, she texted Fran to see if she minded him coming along. Fran's answer was "The more the merrier."

So Jess and Danny met up with Fran, Johnny and Rhys. Fran's sister, Kyra, came along too. Jess was relieved how easily they all fell into chatting. Johnny and Rhys were both incredibly funny and generous when it came to including her dad.

Danny got up to leave around 10.00 p.m., telling Jess to stay on with her friends, but she told him she was going home with him. She'd already told Fran she wasn't going to leave him alone on this, their first Christmas without her mum.

Christmas morning marked the start of their new traditions, and they ate bagels with cream cheese and smoked salmon, and drank Buck's Fizz for breakfast. Kate rarely ate fish, so it wasn't something they would normally have, but both of them loved salmon, so it was an obvious choice.

Afterwards, working their way through a bottle of wine, they opened the few presents they had. Danny bought Jess the new trainers he'd seen her lusting over when they'd last been to town, and book tokens because he knew she never had enough books. Jess bought Danny a jumper and a bottle of single malt whisky, although she wasn't sure the latter was a good present, as in her mind, he'd been drinking a little too much recently. Fran had given Jess a new lippy like the one she used, knowing that Jess wanted the same one. She'd given Fran a decorative heart with words about friendship. Jess tried hard not to think about what Lukas would be doing, and what he might have bought for her, had they still been seeing each other.

In between Christmas and New Year, Jess and Danny went for a lot of walks along the coast. The weather was often cold, and with the sound of the sea and the wind, they didn't have to talk too much. Walking was a good way to be together without speaking, and it seemed both were lost in their own thoughts.

One evening between Christmas and New Year, their neighbours Alison and Paul invited them around for drinks. A few other people from the cul-de-sac were there too, including Anna from the café. Some neighbours had brought their kids with them, but they were much younger than Jess. She chatted to them for a while, mostly asking them what they'd had for Christmas, but she soon got bored. In the end, happily enough, she sat in a quiet corner with her earbuds in. Having such long hair, she could quite easily hide them. It was an interesting place to sit and 'people watch'. Her dad included. He seemed to get on very well with Anna, and Jess wondered if they'd met before. She'd have to remember to ask him.

Eventually noticing that Jess wasn't as engaged in the evening as he was, Danny suggested they go home. They thanked Alison and Paul for a lovely evening and returned next door. The evening hadn't been all bad, and no one had asked her awkward questions, so it could have been far worse.

New Year's Eve was another hurdle for them both. Again, they went to the pub to meet up with Jess' friends. The pub had an extension of opening hours, so they stayed until midnight, celebrating with hugs all round. Jess had no time to think about the past; the present was too busy and too loud. Around twelve thirty, both very tipsy, they went back home and crawled into their beds.

Jess knew her dad was relieved that Christmas was over. She was grateful that her new friends had helped hugely in keeping them both entertained. She'd certainly felt far more relaxed, and she suspected she looked it too. As far as her dad knew, she hadn't had any bad dreams of late. She reckoned he was hoping things had calmed down in the 'ghost' department. But he was wrong.

Alone in her room, Jess had been talking to Amy. She had appeared to her a few times, although, recently, not in her dreams. They'd held conversations where Jess spoke aloud, and Amy answered inside Jess' head. It was a weird sensation, but Jess could always hear her quite clearly. She could physically see her, but for some reason, Amy couldn't actually speak to her out loud. But it didn't matter. Jess had been able to tell Amy about Will's death, and Amy had shared stories of her and Will's happy life together.

A few days into the new year, Jess met Fran and Kyra in the Walkers Rest Café. Once they all had their drinks, they sat at what had become 'their' table near the window. Kyra had a notebook, and Jess had brought the folder with her that she'd been using to make notes about Amy and Will.

"Tell me what you've found out so far," Kyra began.

"I know that they were on the *Aliciana* in 1915 when it sank. Will went down on the ship after being murdered. Amy lived until 1958 in the house we now live in. That's what started all of this." She looked up at Kyra, wanting to see how she was reacting. Kyra was listening intently, without any expression, so she continued. "Then I started having these dreams about Amy during the time the ship sank. So, Dad spoke to a friend of my mum's, who is a medium, and she told him that we must have a spirit in the house. So, the next thing he did was to look up who had lived and died in our house. He came up with Amy. Then we found a locket under the floorboards, and there was a picture I recognised as Amy."

"Then Amy is a ghost, right?" Kyra asked, without any hint of disbelief or sarcasm.

"Yes. You believe me?"

Fran cut in. "Don't you remember me saying that my mum believes in ghosts? So Kyra is used to her."

"Also," Kyra continued, "if you were able to find proof that Amy lived in your house and that she is the same person who was on the ship, then, what's not to believe?"

Jess sighed with relief. Someone was actually believing her. She smiled at Kyra.

"The next thing that happened was I dreamt about Will, Amy's husband, being killed. And the most incredible thing, I had seen a picture of the man who did it, in a house in Anglesey."

"Recently?" Kyra asked.

"Yes. My b—" Jess corrected herself. "A friend took me to visit his grandfather, and the photo was of his father, who was part of the crew on the *Aliciana*. And is considered a hero by the family."

"What was his name?" Kyra asked.

"Peter, I think, but his son – my friend's grandfather – is Sir Robert Anderson."

Kyra looked at her in disbelief. "Okay. That makes things interesting."

"What do you mean?" Jess asked.

"Don't you know who Sir Robert Anderson is?"

"No. Should I?"

"Well, he is one of the owners, and the father of Andersson Global's CEO."

Jess still didn't know who they were but was surprised that Kyra seemed to think she should. Kyra explained that Andersson Global had a great reputation for supporting overseas projects, to build wells in Africa and other countries where water was at a premium.

Lukas' grandfather did seem wealthy, and obviously, Lukas' family wasn't poor either, considering the car he drove. But she'd not ever considered how wealthy he was. She was only interested in him, not his money.

Kyra continued. "I'll see what I can find out about Sir Robert's father, and what his job was on the *Aliciana*."

"Something that might help you. On his cap, he had a large 'M' above the peak."

"Okay. I'll start checking it out for you. If I find anything that relates to an 'M', then at least you'll know you were seeing something based in truth. Was he wearing the cap in the photo you saw of him at Sir Robert's house?"

"No, but I recognised him straight away, the second time I dreamt about him. I knew it was him, but don't know how I can prove it."

"What do you want to happen?" Kyra asked.

Jess was quiet while she considered this. "I'm not sure, but I think I just want to tell Amy why her husband was killed." She looked up at Kyra, who had been interested in everything she'd said. She hadn't once questioned her sanity or laughed at her.

Jess went on. "When I first spoke to Amy, she told me that when she died, she'd expected to join Will on the 'other side'. But, when she got there, she couldn't find him. She didn't understand why, and also, she can't rest or leave this earth until she knows what happened to him. I suppose that sounds really stupid to you?"

"No. There are many things we don't understand in this world, and death is just one of them. I'll find out what I can." Kyra stood up. "Sorry, I've got to get a move on. I've got to get back to Liverpool, so I'll get in touch with you as soon as I find anything." She kissed Fran and gave Jess a hug goodbye.

Fran and Jess remained in the café for another drink, which Jess went to get. "Thanks, Fran, I'm so grateful to you for asking Kyra to help. Sorry, too, that I didn't talk to you much before Christmas. I couldn't talk about what happened with me and Lukas. I still can't, to be honest. I think I've definitely blown it."

"It doesn't help that his great-grandfather seems to be involved, does it?"

"No, it doesn't. And I hadn't appreciated how important his grandfather was either. He's not particularly nice, a bit prickly and full of his own importance. Not at all like Lukas."

"Have you heard from him? Lukas...?" Fran asked.

"No. I don't know if I'm going to."

"Don't give up. You never know what's going to happen."

~

A few days later, Jess' mobile rang. It was Lukas' number. For a short time, she just looked at it but then answered. "Hi."

"Hi, how was your Christmas? Are you okay?" Lukas asked.

"Sort of. Me and Dad made some new traditions for ourselves, you know, the first one without Mum."

"Yeah, I know. It must have been hard."

"It was. Anyway, I'm sorry about when you were here. I didn't mean to scare you away. How was your Christmas?"

"Okay too. I'm going to see the old man again next week. I'll drop by and see you if that's okay?"

Jess was relieved. He wanted to see her again.

"Have you had any more of your dreams over Christmas?" Lukas continued.

"No."

"That's good. I still can't help wondering...perhaps it's all linked in with grief for your mum? It's a huge thing, losing a parent."

Jess' feeling of relief quickly disappeared. "I told you before, they're nothing to do with Mum. They are what they are, but if you don't believe me, you don't. I can't make you believe me."

There was a long silence.

Then Lukas replied, "I'm sorry, Jess, but I just can't rationalise what you are saying. You can't dream truths, you just can't."

Jess took a deep breath, taking her time to answer him. Now was the time to tell him the truth she hadn't told him before. That she had been talking to a ghost called Amy, and another ghost, Will, her husband, had shown her how he had died. The fact that his family was involved just made matters worse, but she had to explain. She took another deep breath and began. "Our house is haunted, and Amy, who I told you about, talks to me—"

Before she could say another word, Lukas cut in. "I don't believe in ghosts, Jess. I've been kind to you. I haven't made any comments about you being off your head or mad. But this... taking the word of something you are seeing in a dream. How do you expect me to accept this Jess? It's not real. It's a dream!"

Lukas ended the call before Jess could answer him.

"Lukas..." Jess buried her head in the nearest pillow and screamed.

14
LLANEIRW, JANUARY 2019

During the first few weeks of the new year, Jess had no direction. Her life seemed aimless. Her dad was still busy renovating the house, having moved upstairs to work on his own room. He had also started running regularly, which kept him out of the house for a couple of hours each day. Jess took the time to write her blog about the experience of moving into Amy's house, without mentioning anything about ghosts.

Jess had been writing blogs for nearly a year. Not every week, but occasionally, sharing her feelings about grief after losing her mum and about moving away from friends and family. She wrote the basic story about Amy and Will McKenzie travelling from America, returning to Manchester. About Amy's survival, her moving to live by the sea, and how, apparently, she had never lost her love for Will in all those years. Living alone by the sea that had taken him from her. She also talked about finding the locket under the floorboards, which contained Amy's photo and a lock of hair with a photo she assumed must have been of Will. Not wanting to say anything about her dreams, she just mentioned that Will's body had never been found and was thought to have gone down with the ship. She took a photo of the locket with her phone, including the two photos inside, and added it to her blog, which she called, 'Amy Unearthed'. She clicked 'Share' and signed off.

A few days later, on one of her days off, a very excited Fran came around to see her. She'd heard from Kyra and had printed off the information she'd sent. Jess read the information with growing excitement. The 'M' on the cap stood for 'Marconi'. Kyra had also written that during the First World War, the Marconi company trained all of the wireless operators who were in the Royal Navy. Due to the outbreak of war, all the Marconi-trained wireless operators were taken off merchant ships and transferred to the Royal Navy. Then, because this left the merchant navy short of wireless operators, Marconi also set up training for those men.

Fran, who was reading the information over Jess' shoulder, excitedly said, "That proves that Lukas' great-grandfather was a Marconi man."

"Yes, but it doesn't prove that it was him who murdered Will. It just proves that I saw him in my dream. That's not truth when he's been dead for so long."

Kyra had also checked the names of crew on the *Aliciana*, and there were two Marconi wireless operators. Peter Anderson and Jack Belton. Further searches for victims showed that Jack Belton was also lost when the ship went down, although he'd managed to send out an SOS just after the ship was hit by the torpedo. Jess was disappointed. The fact that Peter Anderson lived didn't prove to anyone either way if he was the murderer or not.

"Don't be so fed up."

"But that's not proof. How can I prove that someone I've seen in my sleep did murder Will? I just definitely know that he was a Marconi man. I feel like I've hit a dead end." All the excitement she'd initially felt when Fran said there was news had completely disappeared. “I’m sorry. Please thank Kyra for me,” Jess added, not wanting to sound churlish.

When Fran left, Jess walked to the bridge with her and then dropped into the café to pick up a takeaway coffee. She was surprised to see her dad chatting away to Anna.

“I thought you were out running?” she asked.

Danny looked a bit guilty, and Jess wondered why.

“I stopped in for a coffee on the way home. Having a catch-up with Anna while I’m here.”

“I didn’t know you knew Anna that well, although I did notice you chatting at the Christmas do at the neighbours’.”

“Yes, that was the first time we met, and we found a lot to talk about. I often drop in after my run. I need the caffeine.” Danny smiled sheepishly.

After ordering her takeaway, Jess left the café, with a quick glance back. Her dad and Anna seemed to be on very good terms with each other. He’d obviously been there far more often than he had suggested.

As it was a fairly bright day, Jess took her coffee and found the seat near Amy’s grave. Instantly, she could feel Amy’s presence. She told her about her disappointment at only confirming what she already knew – Peter Anderson was on the *Aliciana*. However, she still couldn’t prove it was he who killed Will. Amy was the perfect ‘listening ear’ and Jess could ramble on, and Amy listened. She understood how odd she might look to anyone watching her, as she sat on her bench, between the gravestones, evidently talking to herself.

A couple of days later, still smarting from her disappointment, Jess received an email from someone called Lucy Williams. Lucy had been following her blog. Jess read the email with growing excitement.

> Hi Jess,
> You don't know me, but I've just read your fantastic blog, 'Amy Unearthed', and I think I might be able to help you with some information. My great-grandfather, Hobson Ward, knew someone called Peter Anderson. They were friends. My great-grandfather died a few years after the end of the 2nd World War, although he didn't actually fight himself, due to a medical condition. Knowing how ill he was, he left a letter for his wife, Maud – my great-grandmother – and in it he tells her about Peter – which is the bit I think you'll find very interesting. My great-grandfather says that Peter killed Will.

Lucy wrote a few more things, which Jess skimmed through, including how she'd come across the letter in her Grandma Ivy's possessions when she died. Jess couldn't believe what she'd read. She scanned down to the bottom of the email to see an attachment. She clicked on it, and a handwritten letter appeared in front of her.

Jess started to read the letter. It was quite long, but she hoped it was going to give her some proof about Will's murder and death. The letter was dated June 8th 1944, a year before the Second World War ended.

Dearest Maud,

If you are reading this, my love, then this illness has done for me.

I have managed to reach my fiftieth year, but I know I am not going to be around for many more. There are things I need to share with you, my love. Things I am not proud of and this war has made me question my choices in life. Now I realise my time is short, you need to know the real man you married.

One night in 1913, I met a very young merchant seaman called Peter in a pub near Liverpool docks, where I worked at the time. After quite a few drinks, we had already become chums. He told me he was from Sweden and his name was Per Andersson. He had fled his country after getting into a fight with some Jews, nearly killing one of them. After several more beers, he told me he instigated the attack because they were 'filthy Jews'. Because he was wanted by the police, at the age of 16, he had run away to sea, then changed his name to Peter Anderson, a more acceptable anglicised version of his own. His English was very good, and I suppose, having worked at sea for some time, he had picked up different accents that had eradicated some of his own.

Wow, that wasn't something Jess had expected. That Peter Anderson had attacked someone before. She read on.

As the evening progressed, the beer loosened his tongue further and he began to talk about his hatred for the

Jews, also how sad he was to see so many immigrants here in England.
He was right, at that time, there was quite a lot of nationalist feeling and concern about outsiders getting the jobs that we thought should be ours. In Peter's case, his father was a devout Lutheran and he raised his son with those values. It seemed some Swedes followed the teachings of Martin Luther who, although it had been hundreds of years before, called for the destruction of synagogues and Jewish teachings. Incredibly, his father still held these beliefs. There was also some unrest in Sweden because, like here, the arrival of more foreigners, including Jews, had been perceived by some as competition for jobs. Peter had taken all of this to heart, especially as it supported the views of his father. This all fuelled his anti-Semitic thinking. At the time of our meeting, Peter was two years younger than me, and at nineteen I should have recognised the evil that filled him already at such a young age.
I must add, Maud, I did not have a particular grudge against the Jews, but until I held the job I had in the port, it seemed I was always beaten to every job I applied for by someone who was not English.
When WW1 broke out just a year later, and I am certainly not proud of this, my love, I joined the Empire Action Party. Quite a few people in the group were anti-Semitic, although as I have said, I did not feel strongly about that one way or another. However, I did not see why our government should be spending money to support a war that was started due to an assassination in Europe. Honestly, though, I think the main reason was because that's when doctors picked up on my underlying heart defect, which I now know is far more serious than either

they or I had realised. 'Unfit for service,' they'd said. Being unable to be conscripted made me angry, especially when all my other friends from home were going off to fight. I know it is no excuse, but I felt hard done by and was looking for a group where I belonged.

Initially, the group just started fights and set about anyone they did not like the look of, Jews, or foreigners. However, I am not going to share all the things we did, because I am too ashamed, and I know you are probably already reeling in shock, having read so far.

Maud, I beg you, please don't let what you have read change your thoughts of the man you have loved for the last twenty-four years. Believe me when I say, the things I'm revealing here are the only things I have kept from you.

Even though I did not fully agree with his ideas, Peter and I stayed chums, although we did not manage to meet up again until after the tragic sinking of the *Aliciana*, on which he had been working as part of the crew.

I was quite proud of him too, because it seemed he had changed his whole outlook and had helped people escape into the lifeboats, saving many people's lives. He was being talked about as a hero.

I met with him for a drink around September time, when he was about to leave the merchant navy. I wanted to buy my heroic friend a drink, although other people in the pub beat me to it. So much so, he had drinks piled up in front of him. Surprisingly, he did not want to talk about how he had helped people escape the sinking. Like on our previous meetings, the more he drank, the more freely he talked. As you know, I do not drink that much, so I clearly remember everything he told me.

He surprised me by asking if I had ever killed anyone. Of

course, I told him I had not as I had not fought in the war. Peter had smiled at me. Then almost bragging, told me, he had.

I thought he was talking about the Jew in Sweden who he had injured when he was younger and that he had, in fact, died. He informed me that was not who he was talking about. I began to wonder how he had killed someone when he was in the merchant navy. So, I assumed he must have got involved in another fight, so I asked him.

What he told me is the information that I have carried with me for all of these years and this is the part I am most ashamed of.

Peter told me he had killed a passenger who was on the *Aliciana*. I questioned him about why and how, and he told me the passenger had seen him do something he shouldn't have done. Telling me this, he had a wry smile on his face, as though he had actually enjoyed killing the man.

Jess stopped reading. Here was the proof she'd been looking for. Hobson had to be talking about Will. She read on, hardly daring to breathe.

Unable to fathom what on earth would cause such a terrible consequence and reaction, I asked him, "What did he see you do?"

"He saw me knock out the other radio operator and tear up a message we had received from Admiralty." Peter said this with great pride, as though it was a perfectly normal event.

"How did you kill him?" I'd asked.

"I stabbed him several times; he wasn't going to escape and warn anyone."

Shocked, I asked, "Why did you do that?"

He gave me another wry smile. I could not believe that no other members of the crew had seen this happen, or found the body.

"Surely someone found out?" I'd said.

"No, because about half an hour later or so, the German torpedo hit the boat. I was safe on deck by then."

While I sat listening to him, my own throat had become dry, and I felt sick. Could I believe what he was telling me? Why did he destroy a message from Admiralty? The answer I arrived at back then did not bear thinking about. If you had met him, my love, I am not sure you would have been able to tell truth from lies either. There was always something so evasive about him, and yet he was happily sharing this information with me.

I thought if I asked him the passenger's name, he wouldn't be able to tell me, but he did. Will McKenzie.

Jess gasped. Yes, this was it! Peter killed Will. She read on, wanting to know why he had killed him.

By now, I knew Peter was sly, and probably could invent someone, but the name sounded too plausible not to be true.

I asked him again, "Why did you kill him?"

His reply was to tap the side of his nose, suggesting it was a secret, and he took another swig of his beer.

I must have looked as white as a sheet, and I remember my hand shaking as I picked up my glass to have another sip of my own beer. Peter had been watching me closely. He suddenly changed his complete demeanour and started laughing.

"Can you not recognise a maritime tall tale when you hear one?" he'd asked, continuing to laugh.

I remember I laughed, nervously to start with, but then began to feel incredibly relieved. I couldn't believe that he was that evil. That this young man sitting opposite me could have been responsible for the loss of nearly twelve hundred lives. Could he?

Afterwards, I kept thinking back to the conversation, but I prevaricated too long. I did not do anything about it. I could and should have reported him to the authorities there and then. I did not and I will never know why. However, sometime later, I happened to see a list of the victims lost on the *Aliciana*, and to my horror, there was a William McKenzie. I knew then that Peter had been telling the truth. Of course, by then it was too late to report him, and I was a coward too, because I knew that I would be in trouble for not reporting it sooner.

My love, this is the burden I have kept for all these years. I regret the disappointment you must now feel for me, and I am deeply remorseful. I pray you will be able to forgive me. Hopefully, as you are now reading this and I am dead, you will feel able to share it with the pertinent authorities, should you want to.

I have always been grateful for finding you, my love, and I regret not sharing this with you a long time ago. Know I love you and our children above all else, even after death.

With my deepest respect and love.
Yours always,
Hobson

Jess took her eyes off the screen. She wondered how Maud had reacted after reading this letter from her husband. Wiping the tears from her eyes, that she hadn't even been aware of until now, she shouted out to her dad.

"Dad, where are you?"

Jess kept screaming his name until a worried-looking Danny appeared in her room.

"What's the matter, love?"

"I have the proof that Peter Anderson murdered Will. It's here in a letter that someone has sent me by email. Look."

Danny walked over to her desk and looked at the email. "How do you know it's not a joke? Why would someone send you this?"

"I've been writing a blog, and this girl, Lucy, read it."

"I didn't know you wrote a blog?"

"Yeah. I started writing just after Mum's accident. I got a lot of support from people online who read it."

Danny looked hurt. Noticing, and realising what she had suggested, Jess said, "You were grieving too, so we were in our own worlds." Jess continued. "Anyway, the exciting thing is, Lucy's great-grandfather knew Peter Anderson."

"How do you know she's not just made this up to make you feel better?" Danny asked.

"Because I didn't mention anything about Peter. I just said that I didn't know what happened to Will, because he went down with the ship."

Danny was quiet for a while. "Let me read it."

While he was reading, Jess' mind was working overtime. She

now had her proof, but she still didn't completely understand why he would have killed Will. What did it matter if he saw a message from Admiralty? Why would he care? It didn't make any sense to her.

Having finished reading, Danny looked up at her. "How do you feel about this? After all, it's Lukas' great-grandfather we're talking about here."

"I know. He's who I saw in my dreams, but I couldn't prove it was him, and anyway, Lukas didn't believe me at all. He hasn't spoken to me for ages. I don't know how I'm going to be able to show him this."

"Maybe you could ask Kyra to do some more digging about Peter's background?" Danny said, adding, "I'll pay for her time if needed."

Jess hugged him. "Thank you. That's a great idea. I'll give Fran a ring to find out when she's home again. And I'll thank Lucy for sharing the letter with me. I won't tell her anything else at the moment, but this makes it all seem more real."

15

Following the initial excitement after reading Lucy's letter, nothing else seemed to happen to move things forward. The days ran into each other and generally most days the weather matched the mood: dull. Jess was lazing around in her room. She hadn't heard from Lukas since their last call, but after thinking about it for some time, decided to text him. She wanted him to know about the Marconi cap she'd seen in her dream, and that some research had found that Peter Anderson was one of two Marconi radio operators on the *Aliciana*. At least he would know that she definitely wasn't mad or making it up. But, listening to her dad's advice, she didn't mention the letter she'd received from Lucy.

As soon as she'd texted Lukas, she wished she hadn't, but as she didn't receive a reply, she assumed it had probably done nothing to help her cause either way.

Feeling unsettled, she grabbed her latest book and sprawled out on her bed to start reading. She preferred real books to reading on Kindle, loving the smell, the tactile quality of turning pages, plus you could almost cuddle a book. As she read, she was aware of Danny moving around downstairs and decided to keep out of his way. Unlike her, he'd been far too cheerful over the last few weeks. Jess wondered what had got into him.

~

Danny was fed up with her moping around the house. As much as he loved having her at home, he wished he could do something to cheer her up. Maybe he'd done completely the wrong thing by moving them to Llaneirw, but he knew he couldn't have stayed in Liverpool. Trying to alleviate his selfish feelings, he reminded himself that in September she'd go off to uni, and he'd probably not see her at all. She'd be off out into the world, making her own decisions, without giving him a second thought.

"I bet I know what you're thinking, Katie...I'm making a right pig's ear of all of this. I can't get my head around things without you. You were so much better at this than me."

He had spoken out loud without thinking, and embarrassed, looked around, in case Jess was in earshot. He didn't want her to think he'd turned to the 'woo-woo' side.

He decided a run would clear his head. He needed a break from renovating and decorating. The kitchen and lounge were finished, but there were still a few places that needed a quick touch-up of paint. He'd even replaced the ugly main bathroom too. Now all he needed was to finish his suite on the top floor. He sighed at the thought.

After changing into his running gear, Danny ran out, shouting goodbye to Jess.

~

Although she'd been deeply engrossed in her book, Jess looked at her mobile. She suddenly remembered she'd agreed to meet up with Fran to do some more research. Feeling brighter at the thought of seeing Fran, she perked up even more, remembering she hadn't told her about the email from Lucy. Fran would be just as excited as she was.

When Jess was ready, she went downstairs and was surprised Danny wasn't around. She hadn't heard him go out. She and Fran would probably eat at the pub, so she left him a quick note on the kitchen top as she'd forgotten to tell him she wouldn't be home till late. He was old enough to look after himself, and anyway, he could join them if he wanted to. She smiled.

They'd decided to go to Bangor University library. Fran had told her she liked the buzz there, and that, unlike the local library, there were areas where you could have a quiet conversation without being yelled at.

During the bus journey, Jess excitedly told Fran about Lucy's email. On hearing the news, as Jess had expected, Fran was equally pleased.

At the library, they used Jess' laptop to research Peter Anderson's background. However, the only information they found was about his 'heroism' as a crew member of the *Aliciana,* and quite a bit about him setting up his business, Anderson Pumps. The latter was pretty boring, Jess had to be honest. Oddly, there didn't seem to be any reference to his Swedish background.

Fran suggested they should try Ancestry.com to see if they could find Lukas' Swedish ancestors. However, they hadn't realised how much information would be needed, even just to start a search. They needed to know the person's date of birth, where they lived, and names of other family members, about which they knew next to nothing. However, despite their lack of information, it appeared there was a database of birth records from 1859 to 1947, which would probably have been very useful – had they known anything. Plus, they would have to pay a subscription too. They delved a little further and found that, unlike British names, there was an added complication with Swedish names.

Reading the information together, they discovered that surnames seemed to change a lot, and initially couldn't understand why a Nils Larsson and his father, Lars Eriksson, didn't have the same surname. Searching further, it seemed that Swedish surnames were patronymic names. Johansson was the son of Johann, and Eriksson, the son of Erik. It was similar with girls too. They also took their father's name, so Ander's daughter Agnes became Agnes Andersdotter, and Klara Hansdotter was the daughter of Hans. This meant that male and female siblings would have similar but different surnames. Because of this patronymic system, the surname often changed with each generation. So, Nils Larsson was the son of Lars Eriksson, and Lars was the son of Erik Andersson and so on.

"Oh my God, that's seriously over-complicated," said Fran.

"Yeah, mental. It's doing my head in," Jess answered, scanning the next paragraph.

"Hey, but not all bad, at least when a Swedish woman got married, she kept her own name. That would make things easier compared to today. One of the nurses at work who got married recently was complaining about having to inform so many different people, like banks, driving licence," Fran said.

"Yeah, it makes a change to read about women keeping control of their names. I hate the way we always have to change our surnames if we marry."

Jess scanned through the information. "It says here that the Swedes stopped the patronymic system in 1901 when people had to adopt heritable surnames that could be passed down generations." She paused to think about something. "That's going to make it hard to find any information about Per Andersson, because with that weird system, there must have been loads of Anderssons."

Fran nodded at Jess, who was feeling disheartened by what they'd found.

"Look, let's leave this for today. We won't be able to find anything, but I bet I know a girl who can."

"Do you really think Kyra would help us with this, Fran?"

"I'm sure she would. I bet she'll have some contacts who have contacts in Sweden, who could help us find out more. Anyway, can't you just ask Lukas more about his great-grandfather?"

Jess had briefly felt more optimistic, hearing Fran's words, but she suddenly went quiet. "Mm...He's fallen out with me. I didn't want to tell you, because I'm trying to put him out of my mind."

Jess' eyes filled with tears and Fran glanced at her. "I'm sorry. Why didn't you tell me? Typical guy. What's wrong with him?" She hugged Jess. "Look, let's forget this. Go and get something to eat, have a walk and blow him out of your head. At least for today."

Jess smiled. "Yeah, I'm trying to forget him, honestly."

"Kyra will know where to look far better than us, so don't worry. If there's stuff to find about Peter Anderson, she'll track it down, no problem."

Fran began to clear up her stuff, Jess shut down her laptop, and arm in arm, they went off in search of a snack, as they'd already planned to eat later at The Blue Dolphin.

16

Danny arrived back from his run a lot later than he had expected, mainly because he'd dropped into the café for a coffee and catch up with Anna. He'd walked back from the café in the dark.

At his front door, he turned the key in the lock and was surprised when someone came up behind him and forcibly pushed him into the hall. Danny twisted his arm out of the awkward angle it'd been put in and let go of the key, which was now bent and misshapen in the lock.

"What the hell..." Danny turned to see two men standing behind him, one of them shutting the front door after himself.

"Where's your computer, mate?" the largest of the two men asked.

"What? What are you doing? Get out, or I'm going to call the police." Danny tried to get his mobile out of the belt around his waist, but it wasn't there. *Shit, I must have left it at Anna's*, he thought.

The larger man managed to grab Danny's arm before he could make any moves and twisted it behind his back. Danny groaned in pain. While 'Thug', as Danny was now thinking of him, held him, the second man, who was far slimmer and quieter, was checking in the rooms downstairs. He asked, "Is there anyone else in the house?"

"No."

The man continued. "Where is the research you have been doing about the *Aliciana*?"

Danny couldn't believe what he was hearing. He was relieved Jess wasn't in the house. At least he hoped she wasn't.

"What research?" He tried to sound convincing, though obviously not enough, as Thug pushed Danny's arm upwards into a far more painful position.

"Look, mate, we're not playing around here. We want to know where the computer is with all the information you've got about the *Aliciana*. Okay!"

"I haven't got any information. You can look on my computer, but to be honest, there's nothing on there that you'll find interesting, unless you're into interior design." Danny tried to sound more unconcerned than he was.

Thug pushed Danny up against the wall harder, pressing his face into the newly finished paintwork that he'd spent ages doing. He hadn't expected to see it quite this close up.

The quieter man whispered in his ear. "So, you haven't got the computer here, but if we find out you've been doing any other research, then things will be a lot worse next time we visit. So, keep your nose out of things that don't concern you, and tell that daughter of yours the same. Have you got that?"

Danny panicked when the guy mentioned Jess. He was beginning to feel very intimidated by now. His mind was racing with so many different thoughts about exactly who was behind this, and how they could think they'd get away with it. And again, how grateful he was that Jess wasn't home.

At that moment, there was a thud on the floor upstairs. "You said there wasn't anyone else in the house." Thug gave Danny's arm another push upwards.

Between groans, Danny managed, "There isn't anyone else here."

"So, what was that?"

Suddenly the lights that were on in the lounge and on the landing flickered. They went off completely for a second, and then back on.

"Stop messing us about. Tell whoever it is to stop and come down here." Thug had his face pressed as close as he could to Danny's without actually kissing him.

"I've told you, there's nobody here." Then Danny had a brain-wave. "But we have got a ghost."

Thug slapped Danny with his free hand, hard across his face. The force of the slap hit Danny's head against the wall.

The lights began flickering again, on and off, continuously. The quieter man looked at Thug. "Maybe he's telling the truth. Perhaps they have got a ghost."

"You kidding me, don't be daft. You don't believe that crap, do ya?"

There was a silence as the two uninvited guests glared at each other.

The quieter man was frozen, pointing at the stairs. "I do now. Can't you see her too?"

"Who?" asked Thug.

Danny tried to turn his badly aching head to see who they were talking about.

"Can't you see her? Like a mirage at the top of the stairs. Look." Again, the quieter man pointed at the stairs. "I've had enough of this. Come on, let's leave him."

Thug held his ground, still manhandling Danny. "We're here

to do a job. I'm not leaving until we find what we came for. Don't be such a wimp."

At that exact moment, the doorbell rang. Danny struggled to get from under Thug's body and arms and managed to make use of the element of surprise afforded by the ringing bell to wriggle free a little. Thug grabbed him and put his hand over Danny's mouth while Danny still tried to free himself from his vice-like grip. The person ringing the bell was impatient, and knocking on the door, shouted Danny's name.

The quieter man turned to Thug and said, "That's it, I'm making a move. We don't want others involved."

He opened the door and pushed past a very surprised Anna, knocking her onto the grass. Thug released his grip on Danny, pushing him away. Danny fell awkwardly, due to his twisted arm, and as he fell, he hit his head on the bottom step.

The two thugs disappeared as suddenly as they'd arrived.

Jess and Fran had just finished their meal and were having another drink when they heard the siren. Everyone in The Blue Dolphin heard it too, and several rushed outside to see where it was, because it was obviously close. Someone came back in and said, "It's a few houses down."

Anxiously, Jess rushed out of the pub, closely followed by Fran, who had grabbed their coats and bags. They arrived at Number 17 in time to see Danny being put into the ambulance, and a police car parked alongside. Anna, who'd been talking to one of the paramedics, rushed over to Jess as soon as she saw her. Anna held Jess back from climbing into the ambulance, where Danny was hidden by the two paramedics still tending to him.

"Don't panic. They're taking care of him, and the police are in the house checking things out."

"What happened?" Jess was bewildered. Why were the police there? What was going on?

"I came around to drop your dad's mobile off. He'd left it in the café earlier. After I rang the bell, two men ran past me, knocking me over, and then I found Danny on the floor, so rang for an ambulance."

"Dad!" Jess pulled away from Anna and, again, started towards the ambulance, but this time it was Fran who held her back.

"They're just treating him at the moment. Wait until they're ready. Then you can go with him."

Jess' mind was racing, instantly going back to her mum's accident. This was like déjà vu. The same feeling of helplessness and a sudden sinking in her stomach hit her hard. She was unable to catch her breath and everything around her started to go black. Feeling strong arms around her, through the blackness, she could faintly hear someone speaking.

"You're okay. Just breathe." One of the paramedics helped her to sit on the wall. He handed her a glass of water that Fran had been to get.

"Do you want to go in the ambulance along with your dad?" he asked.

"Please. He's going to be okay, isn't he?"

"He's had a very bad bump to his head, but we'll know more when we get to hospital. He's unconscious at the moment, so we need to get going."

"Can my friend Fran come with me, please?" Jess asked.

"No, I'm sorry, only you can go with your dad. She can follow on and meet you there."

Anna said, "Don't worry, I'll bring Fran with me. We'll be with you soon."

"What about the house...and the police?" Jess asked.

"I'll speak to them. We won't leave the house unlocked. You go. Don't worry about this. We'll see you soon," Anna said.

Jess left Fran and Anna as the ambulance, siren blaring, went off into the night.

17

Fran and Anna found Jess sitting forlornly on her own in a corridor outside A & E, waiting to hear news. When she saw Fran and Anna, she burst into tears. Once she was calmer, Jess told them they hadn't told her anything yet, but the doctor had said he would come back to give an update as soon as possible.

Anna went off to get them cups of tea and coffee, during which time the doctor came out to see Jess.

"Okay. Your dad has got a dislocated shoulder, which we have dealt with, but the serious issue is the head injury he received. We are concerned about some brain swelling, so we have put him in a medically induced coma."

Jess panicked and he put a hand on her shoulder, quickly adding, "It is only temporary to allow his body to heal. He's stable for now, and over the next few days, we'll keep a close watch over him in the intensive care unit."

Tears streamed down Jess' face, but she made no noise.

"Can I see him?" she managed to ask.

"Yes, for a short time only, but of course you can."

The doctor called a nurse over, and she led Jess into the room where Danny lay surrounded by beeping machines, wires and drips. He had a breathing tube in his mouth, and his head was bandaged. Seeing him like this, Jess couldn't help but cry out and step backwards. The nurse gently put her arm around her.

"It always looks a lot worse than it is, love. Everything you see is helping him and keeping him safe and calm. Hold his hand gently, and talk to him."

Jess gingerly moved towards the bed and carefully touched his hand.

"Hi, Dad." She sniffed back her tears. "You don't look your best, but I'm happy to see you safe and alive." She looked back at the nurse, feeling awkward, not knowing what to say.

"Why don't we leave him to rest for now? You can come back in the morning when you've had some sleep and feel calmer yourself too."

The nurse led her from the room and back into the waiting arms of Fran.

Anna handed Fran the car keys. "Take Jess back to the car and I'll catch up in a sec."

After watching them disappear down the corridor, Anna spoke to the nurse. She wanted to make sure that Danny really was okay and that they weren't playing his condition down to keep Jess calm. Placated by the answers, she found her way back to the car park to drive them all home.

When they arrived back, there was still a police car outside the house. After telling Fran to take Jess inside, Anna went to talk to the policemen on duty. They told her they were going to stay outside for the rest of the night, which wasn't that long anyway, and they'd leave when the locksmith came by in the morning.

Fran glanced at her friend with her tear and make-up-streaked face, sitting clutching a cushion against her body. She was obviously still in shock, so Fran rang her mum, who was none too happy being woken in the middle of the night. However, she understood why, when Fran explained the reason she was going to stay with Jess.

Anna came into the house and told Fran what the police had said. She asked if they wanted her to stay too. Jess didn't answer, but Fran told her they'd be fine on their own, especially with the police car outside.

After Anna left, Fran shut the front door behind her and pushed the hall table against it – just in case. *In case of what?* she thought, realising how flimsy it would be if someone was serious about getting inside the house. But, again, knowing the police were outside was some comfort.

When she went back into the lounge, Jess was in exactly the same spot she'd left her. "Do you want to go upstairs to sleep, or do you want to go to sleep down here?" Fran asked.

Jess looked surprised that someone had spoken to her. "Er... Down here I think." She looked around helplessly.

Fran knew that nothing she said would help Jess, but from her training, she knew to keep Jess warm and to encourage her to get some sleep.

"I'll make us a warm drink, and then we'll see if we can both get some sleep. Okay?"

Absently, Jess nodded.

After finishing their drinks, Fran persuaded Jess to put her feet up on the sofa, and she went upstairs for Jess' duvet, which she wrapped around her. Then Fran found a warm blanket for herself on one of the other chairs and tucked her feet up, snuggling into the chair, ready for sleep.

Around 8.00 a.m., Fran and Jess were woken by someone knocking on the front door. Fran told Jess to stay where she was, and after moving her table barricade, opened the door to the locksmith who had come to put a new lock on the front door.

Fran had a hard time persuading Jess to eat anything but eventually managed to get her to have a piece of toast and a hot drink. "Did you manage to sleep much last night?" she asked Jess.

"Some, but everything kept going over in my mind. Who would attack Dad? He hasn't done anything to anyone, and he doesn't know that many people here either. It just doesn't make any sense."

"Don't worry about that. The police will be looking into it," Fran answered, although she didn't believe the police would come up with much. No one had seen anything, and with Danny in a coma, he wasn't going to be able to help either.

"Do you want to have another sleep, or take a shower and go over to the hospital?" Fran asked.

"What?"

It seemed Jess hadn't heard a word, so Fran repeated her question.

Jess decided a shower might be a good thing. She disappeared upstairs, telling Fran she could manage on her own.

Standing in the shower, Jess began to cry uncontrollably. She slid down the tiles and ended up sitting under the cascade of water, where her tears mingled with the stream.

Jess' mind was racing with images and thoughts about losing Danny. He couldn't die. What would she do without him? She couldn't believe this had happened. It was only just under a year since her mum had died.

"Mum, I need you, and you're not here. What am I going to do? What if Daddy...d-dies too?" Her heart was breaking with worry. She couldn't cope with this too.

Finally, she managed to contain her crying, and, standing, turned off the shower, and in auto mode, dried herself.

Back in her room, as she was dressing, the air stilled. She knew Amy was with her, and turning, saw her standing near the window. She heard her voice.

Don't be scared, Jess. Your dad is still alive. He hasn't crossed over. But, I want you to know I was here last night. I tried to help, but obviously I couldn't do anything physical to the men. I managed to make the lights flicker on and off, and moved some things around so they thought there was someone else in the house. One of them could see me too, which rattled him, and then after the doorbell rang, they ran.

"Oh, Amy. Thank you. Did you hear what they were saying?"

Not really, I'm sorry. I heard your dad cry out, which is why I tried to scare them off.

At that moment, Fran walked into the room. "I heard you talking and wondered if it was the hospital phoning."

"No, it wasn't. I was talking to Amy."

Fran looked around the room. "Is she still here?"

"Yes, she's by the window. Can't you feel the chill in the room?"

Again, Fran looked around. "No, it feels fine to me."

Jess turned back towards the window, but Amy had left. With far more enthusiasm than Fran had seen from her in the last twelve hours or so, Jess seemed encouraged by Amy's visit.

"She tried to help Dad. Would you believe it? She actually tried to help him, and I think it did help. That and the doorbell, which must have been Anna. Amy said that he isn't on the other side."

Fran said she was pleased that Amy had given Jess something positive. She didn't look fully convinced, but Jess suspected it was because she was a trainee nursing associate, so she'd have seen several comas, not all of which would have ended positively. Jess hoped beyond hope that Amy was right and that her dad would survive.

They were interrupted by a knock on the door. The police had come to question Jess to ask if she knew of any reason why her dad might have been attacked. They'd already been around to Anna's to question her, but as she had been knocked over by the two assailants as they'd rushed out of the house, she couldn't even describe them.

Jess answered all she could of the policeman's questions, but he seemed disappointed she couldn't enlighten him any further than Anna had. The police hadn't found any fingerprints, and no one saw anything. Although someone did mention a car parked opposite the houses, which was unusual. But, neither Jess nor Fran had seen it. It'd been dark, and they'd been on the way home from The Blue Dolphin, having had quite a bit to drink, so they hadn't taken much notice. The police said it might be nothing; it could have been a visitor to one of the other houses – they were looking into it. They'd tried to track the two assailants on CCTV along the routes in and out of Llaneirw at that time but had the opinion that they must have been professionals, because they managed to evade being photographed, and some of the number plates were indecipherable.

"We'll keep searching, but we're going to have to wait until your dad wakes up, and hopefully we can question him then. See if he can give us any clues as to who it was who attacked him."

When the police left, as though she had been watching, Anna knocked on the door.

"Would you like a lift to the hospital to see your dad?"

"Oh, are you sure? Who's going to run the café?" Jess asked.

"I'm not worried about that. Danny is more important, and

you don't want to be having to catch buses backwards and forwards. I'm happy to help."

"Okay, thank you then. Fran, are you going home? I'll probably stay at the hospital most of the day. I'll take something to read – if I can concentrate."

"I'll come and stay again tonight, if you want," Fran said.

Jess hugged her friend and set off with Anna.

Arriving at the hospital, Jess spotted the nurse from the previous night and noticed that her name badge said 'Bethan'. She came over to them.

"He's had a good night. Everything is as it should be, and the consultant is happy with his progress so far. Go in and talk to your dad about anything and everything. Imagine he's just listening to you with his eyes shut." Smiling, she gave Jess a gentle, encouraging push towards Danny's room.

Anna followed her in and said, "I'll just come and say hello and then leave you. Ring me when you want me to come over and collect you. Okay?"

Anna walked over to Danny and quietly whispered "Hello." To Jess' surprise, She kissed him on the forehead. Then, without looking back, Anna turned and left, leaving Jess alone with Danny.

Jess pulled a chair up to the bedside and reached out to hold his hand, careful not to touch any of the wires or cannulas. For ages, she just looked at him, not knowing what to say. He looked so vulnerable with the ventilator helping him breathe, and all of the drips and medical paraphernalia around him.

Yet again, she found herself silently crying, and she wiped her face. "Dad, I need you, so just sleep as long as you need so that you heal." She leant in and kissed his hand then laid her head on the bed, next to the hand she was holding.

After a short while, exhausted by crying and having not slept much the night before, Jess fell asleep.

She was woken by Bethan gently shaking her shoulder. "Jess... Jess. We just need to come in and sort some things out for your dad. Why don't you go and get a hot drink and something to eat? Then when you come back, we'll be done, and you can chat to him again."

Jess sat up, stretching her shoulders. "He's alright, isn't he?"

"Yes, we just need to do checks, but they're things we have to do regularly. There's nothing wrong."

Jess took the opportunity to head to the café for a coffee and a chocolate bar. She didn't feel like eating real food, she just needed something sugary.

On her return, her dad looked much the same. She returned to her seat, and this time, she began to talk to him. She told him about the trip she and Fran had taken to Bangor, and all about Amy trying to help him. Then she made a joke about him being sly, asking him what was going on with him and Anna.

By mid-afternoon, Jess was feeling incredibly tired, so she rang Anna to ask her to collect her.

Back at home, knowing Amy was watching over her, Jess felt more secure. Though she knew that if anyone did break in again, Amy couldn't do anything physical. She wasn't corporeal, but she would be able to warn her. Although Amy didn't always reveal herself, Jess knew she was there. She had become a constant in Jess' life.

For the next three days, Jess' life continued in the same routine. Fran came to stay with her overnight, making sure she was eating properly, and then Anna took her to and from the hospital.

According to the hospital, Danny was still okay, and the hospital staff told her he would probably wake up any day soon. Jess prayed they were right. She couldn't lose him too. Her life wouldn't be worth living.

18

Lukas knew there was something special about Jess the first time he met her. He hadn't been thrilled at the idea of showing possible undergrads around the campus. However, she was beautiful, with the most amazing blue eyes, something quite unexpected in a dark-haired person. He had liked everything about her, and even then, he could feel the mutual attraction between them. On that first meeting, she'd seemed fairly well-balanced and knew exactly what she wanted to do with her life. However, after taking her to Anglesey, he no longer thought that was the case. He'd wanted to move things forward and tell her he cared about her, but things had gone downhill fast.

From their first meeting at the open day, they'd kept in touch. After the death of her mum, he had been there to support her with her grief, but when she'd told him about seeing ghosts, had made accusations about his great-grandfather, and had showed him her awful bruise, he hadn't believed her. He couldn't believe her. Nothing he'd done would have given her that bruise, and he knew in his heart that Danny wouldn't have hurt her either. And surely, she didn't do it to herself? To what end? Lukas just didn't know if he could cope with all that baggage. He was used to living a hassle-free life. Did he really want it to change?

When he'd phoned Jess after Christmas, and she'd tried to explain her behaviour in Anglesey, instead of trying to understand, he'd pushed her away. Yet, some of what she'd said stuck with him. He'd begun to question his own beliefs about his great-grandfather and wondered if there was a tangible reason why his dad didn't get on with him.

Today, he had been shocked into considering that maybe she had been telling the truth all the time. Her friend, Fran, had contacted him to tell him that Danny had been attacked and was in a coma. Lukas' mouth filled with bile when he recalled the phone conversation he'd had with his grandfather after visiting Anglesey. Lukas had mentioned how upset Jess had been when she'd seen the photo of his great-grandfather, and he recalled his grandfather's extreme response.

"Why on earth have you aligned yourself to a girl like that?" he'd said.

"What do you mean, Grandfather? Like what?"

"Overly sensitive, and hysterical, of course."

"Jess isn't either of those, Grandfather. But her mum was killed last year, so she's had a bad time. But she's normally level-headed. You remember me telling you she's been doing some research into the *Aliciana*? Well, she found something out about your dad, Peter..."

Sir Robert had interrupted Lukas. "What the hell is she doing researching the *Aliciana*? It has nothing to do with her, and there's nothing to find out about my dad. So, just stop thinking about it. Anyway, where is this girl from? What does her father do?"

At the time, Lukas had noted how abruptly his grandfather had changed the direction of the conversation.

"What has where she comes from got to do with anything, Grandfather? Or what her father does? It's not the Dark Ages, you know. I can date who I like."

"I want to know if you're chasing unsuitable girls, that's all. So, where's she from?"

Lukas remembered shouting at his grandfather, "She's from Llaneirw, and she's perfectly suitable, thank you," before slamming the phone down.

At the time, he'd been so angry at what the old man was insinuating. Plus what had it got to do with him who he dated? His own dad never interfered.

A few weeks later, he'd phoned his grandfather to apologise for slamming the phone down on him, but also in that conversation, he'd talked about Jess seeing his father with a Marconi cap on. His grandfather had sounded very surprised about that and had asked how Jess could have seen that, but Lukas had fudged around the answer.

His grandfather had expressed complete disdain of the idea, asking, "How indeed could she have seen that anywhere? He's not wearing it in the photo she saw in this house."

After going quiet for a few moments, yet again, their conversation had ended rather abruptly. This time, Lukas' grandfather had put the phone down.

Now, sitting in his bedroom in Manchester, Lukas recognised both conversations had perhaps taken a more sinister turn. That he might have been the person to have caused Danny's situation by sharing too much with his grandfather. Lukas knew his grandfather, in his 'Sir Robert' guise, liked to be in control, and he had this terrible foreboding deep inside that he might have given him too much information about Jess.

Lukas leapt up off his bed. He needed to get a grip and give himself a good talking to. He was letting his imagination run away with him. It wasn't as if his grandfather was a gangster.

Was he really the type of man to send people after Danny, just because they were researching the boat his great-grandfather had sailed on? *Stop creating drama!* he said to himself.

He made the decision to grab some clothes and go down to visit Jess. Despite not wanting the baggage, he realised he cared for her far more than he was willing to accept. But he wasn't going to mention his worries about his grandfather – he'd keep that to himself.

After dropping a bag with a few changes of underwear and a different jumper onto the passenger seat of his car, he texted Fran to warn her he was on his way, asking where Jess would be.

Lukas pulled into the Ysbyty Gwynedd hospital car park at Bangor and asked at the reception desk where he might find the ICU. As he walked towards the door of Danny's room, where the nurse had directed him, he could see Jess sitting by her dad's bedside.

"Jess, I'm so sorry..." Lukas began, but before finishing, Jess stood up and threw herself into his arms.

19

Lukas was shocked to see how tired Jess looked, but on reflection, it was understandable; she'd said she'd hardly slept since Danny's attack. When they got back to the house, Lukas dumped his bag in the lounge and offered to make them both a hot drink. Jess threw herself onto the sofa, but by the time Lukas had found where everything was and taken the drink over to her, she was fast asleep. He covered her over with a blanket that was on the back of the sofa and went upstairs into the room where he'd slept when he last stayed over.

He hadn't spoken to his dad since hearing about Danny's attack, so he rang him to tell him that he'd be staying with Jess for a couple of days. Then he texted Fran to tell her he'd arrived and asked if she was free for a quick chat. She told him she could be around at Jess' in a couple of minutes. Lukas told her not to ring the bell, but text him when she arrived.

When Lukas let Fran in, she gave him a smile. He wondered what Jess had told her about him, but now wasn't the time for gossip. Instead, he said, "Jess fell asleep as soon as we got home, on the sofa, so come upstairs and we can chat without waking her."

Sitting in the spare room, Lukas asked Fran to tell him everything she knew about the night of Danny's attack. As he listened, he began to feel more uncertain about his grandfather's involvement and was hoping he might get some hints from what she told him. He was disappointed when Fran explained that the police didn't know anything. They hadn't found fingerprints, no one had seen the men, all cars nearby were accounted for, and, annoyingly, the CCTV didn't catch a good image either.

"How did they manage to evade the CCTV?" Lukas asked.

"It seems they managed to evade being captured full-on by any of the CCTV cameras in the area, so that was no help whatsoever. The police reckon they must have parked on the new town side and walked through the underpass, and that they'd done this sort of thing before. They certainly weren't amateurs."

Annoyed with himself, Lukas actually felt some relief. Even if his over-dramatic thinking was correct, at the moment, nothing could be proved. "How has Jess taken it all?"

"How do you expect? She only lost her mum last year, and she thought she'd lost her dad too. She's trying to keep a brave face, but I know she's not been sleeping well. I've been staying with her for the last week. I presume you'll be staying tonight?"

Thoroughly admonished, Lukas replied, "Yeah, but I can only stay a couple of nights. I'm off to Sweden next week, but only for a couple of days, as part of my uni course."

Fran nodded. "I know it's none of my business, but please don't mess her about, Lukas. She's too fragile at the moment. I know you two fell out, but you obviously care, otherwise you wouldn't be here. Anyway, thanks for coming, and it's good to meet you, after I've heard so much about you."

They heard some movement from downstairs. Jess was moving around and called out, "Lukas, are you still here?"

"Yes, I'll be down, just upstairs."

Fran walked down to the front door, passing Jess, who

looked up from the sofa, surprised to see her. "I'll leave you two in peace."

Lukas went back into the lounge and sat next to a bleary-eyed Jess and pulled her towards him.

"What was Fran doing here?" she asked.

"I wanted her to tell me what happened, while you were sleeping, so you didn't have to hear it all again."

"Thank you. I don't really want to keep thinking about it, but while Dad's still in his coma, it's difficult to relax."

"I know. I can stay with you tonight and tomorrow, but I've got to get back the day after."

Trying to keep her mind off things for a short while, he told her about his fieldtrip to Sweden, which was linked to his degree work. His ploy seemed to work; Jess loved hearing about Sweden.

Later, after eating a meal that Lukas prepared, they sat listening to music together. They didn't talk much, just enjoyed being together in the moment, and neither of them raised the topic of spirits or Jess' dreams.

When the time came for sleep, they walked upstairs, together, and when they reached Jess' room, Lukas pulled her to him. To start with, he kissed her gently on the lips, but as the kiss lingered, his need for her grew. Jess pulled away from him.

"Lukas, you know I want you, don't you? But now isn't the right time. As much as I want to feel your naked body next to mine, and make love, I don't want 'comfort' sex. I want to be fully alive, aware and in the moment. I want it to be anxiety-free, which while I'm continually thinking about Dad, it wouldn't be. I'm sorry."

"No, I'm sorry. I didn't mean to push you." He kissed her gently again.

"You didn't, Lukas, I'm not saying 'no' forever. Just for now. But, please, can we just lie together tonight, so I can feel you holding me? You make me feel safe."

For the next two days and nights, they were inseparable. Lukas was so thankful to Fran for contacting him. He knew he cared deeply for Jess, but now, deep down, there was also this nagging suspicion that his grandfather might have had something to do with Danny's attack, however outlandish an idea it was.

20

LLANEIRW, FEBRUARY 2019

Fran moved back in with Jess after Lukas left, relieved she'd done the right thing in contacting him.

On their next visit, all of Danny's breathing tubes had been removed and he was breathing perfectly well by himself. However, he still hadn't woken up. The doctors were still telling Jess that all of his vital systems were working well, and hopefully he would wake up soon. This wasn't particularly encouraging to Jess, but Fran told her, the fact that he was breathing on his own, and had no issues with his brain functions was good. There was no reason why he wouldn't wake soon. Jess still spent as much time as she could at the hospital, although she was now making sure that she slept and ate. Fran had told her if she made herself ill, she would be no use to her dad when he came home.

Jess had good news when Kyra found some information about Peter Anderson. She emailed it over to her, and she and Fran pored over it together while drinking a glass of wine.

Through her Swedish contact, Kyra had found that Peter Anderson, born Per Andersson in 1896, left his home town of Vaxholm under a cloud, when he was 16, but so far, she couldn't find out what the cloud was. She also found proof that he was on the *Aliciana* as 2nd Marconi operator, and after the First World War, had gone to work for a company that manufactured pumps. Over the years, he'd worked his way up in the company and incredibly had been left the business by the previous owner when he died. By the Second World War, the company was known as Anderson Pumps, and they actually supported the war effort, though little seems to have been known about Peter Anderson at that time. That is, apart from the fact he'd built his life on his reputation as a hero, helping people into lifeboats as the *Aliciana* was sinking. Per's son, Sir Robert, received his knighthood in the mid-80s after taking over the company from his father. He received his knighthood for the company's continuing service, providing jobs and supporting local charity.

"This just proves that Peter was one of the two Marconi operators and that he started the business of Anderson Pumps, but it doesn't tell me how Peter started out as the man that Hobson talks about in his letter," Jess said, clearly disappointed.

Recognising her mood, Fran suggested they ask Kyra to see if she could find out more about why he had to leave Sweden. There must be some record somewhere, surely?

"I'll ask her if her Swedish contact could dig any deeper."

"Thank you, Fran. Dad said he could pay Kyra for her time if she needed it. Though now..."

"Don't be silly. I'm sure she can owe her contact some research in the future. Stop worrying about that for now."

The next day, Jess woke to the sound of her mobile. The hospital was phoning to say Danny had woken up, and she could go in and visit. Fran had left early for work, so Jess rang Anna to tell her because she knew she'd also been going in to visit her dad. Anna offered to drive.

Jess' nerves began to kick in as they approached the hospital. What if there were problems that the medical staff hadn't picked up on? What if he couldn't speak properly, or his mind wasn't fully working? By the time she and Anna arrived at her dad's room, she was feeling physically sick.

Bethan greeted Jess with a big smile. "He's doing really well. He had a little bit to eat and drink earlier, and although his voice is weak, he is talking. Though he doesn't remember much about what happened, so don't push him too much about that. Be gentle with him. Okay?"

Jess walked into her dad's room. He was sitting up, looking unsurprisingly the worse for wear. Definitely better than she'd seen him over the last few days, though. She rushed over and was about to throw her arms around him when she remembered Bethan's words, to be gentle. "Dad..." was all she could manage before her emotions overwhelmed her, and she burst into tears.

Gingerly, with cannulas still attached, he lifted his hand to stroke Jess' cheek. "I'm okay, my lovely. Glad to see you though."

Jess kissed him very gently on his cheek too, being wary of the bandages that he still had around his head. "Anna's here to see you too. Should I fetch her?"

"No, you stay for a little longer, just so I can look at you. Who's been looking after you?"

"I don't need looking after, but it seems you do! Fran stayed with me, and the police had the locks changed, and then Lukas came over to see me."

"So, you've not really had time to miss me then." Danny managed a gentle smile.

"I'm glad to see you've not lost your sense of humour, Dad!"

They sat together and chatted about nothing in particular, just incredibly relieved to see each other. After a while, Jess said she'd go and get a drink, and she waved Anna in to see him. She asked Anna if she wanted a drink too and disappeared off to the café.

When she returned, she was a bit taken aback to see Anna holding her dad's hand, which she hurriedly removed when Jess walked into the room. There was certainly more to their friendship than Jess had realised. She wasn't too sure what her feelings were about this, but today wasn't the time to worry about that.

A week later, Danny was allowed home from the hospital, with instructions to take things easy. Jess rushed around, looking after him, although she ignored doing any real cleaning in the rest of the house, but kept his room clean and tidy, along with the lounge and kitchen. Initially, Danny slept in the lounge as he hadn't got enough stamina to get upstairs. He joked about having to put up with her cooking, which she had to admit, wasn't the best. But he began to build back his strength and was eventually well enough to move back into his own room.

Jess hadn't mentioned her research or her dreams, because she hadn't wanted to worry him, so they just talked about safe things. She wasn't even sure how much he remembered of what had been happening. On good days, they went out along the sea paths for gentle walks, which were lovely as the weather began to get warmer.

At first, he hadn't remembered much about the attack, and Jess had kept her promise to Bethan not to push him. However, the police had contacted her to ask that if Danny did remember anything that would help them in their inquiries, she was to get in touch. So far, her answer had been "Nothing."

While eating tea one evening, Danny suddenly said, "My computer."

"What about your computer?" Jess asked.

"That's what they kept asking me, where my computer was."

"Did they say why?"

"I don't know, maybe, but...I can't remember."

Danny took a few more mouthfuls, then spluttered, "The *Aliciana*. They kept asking where the information was."

Jess went cold. "Do you mean they were asking about information you had on the *Aliciana*?"

Danny looked panicked. "Yes. Oh, God, Jess, they told me to tell you to keep out of it. To stop researching into the *Aliciana*."

Jess was worried, thinking this might make Danny ill in some way, but he looked physically okay. "We have to tell the police, Dad. Do you remember anything about the men who attacked you?"

"Weirdly, not a lot. Just that one was very large, and the other was quietly spoken, but I wasn't bothered what they looked like, when they were trying to break my arm."

"No, I suppose not."

"Jess? I think your lady spirit – I've forgotten her name, tried to help me. Does that sound as mad to you as it does to me?"

"No, you're not mad. Yes, Amy did try to help. She managed to move some stuff around and make them think there was someone else in the house. Then she managed to manifest an apparition that one of them saw, which is partly why they ran off. Amy said they were arguing, and then Anna rang the bell and knocked on the door, and that finally sent them packing."

Danny, looking around the room, said, "I never expected to say this, but, wherever you are, Amy, thank you."

Jess went and hugged Danny. "She knows you're grateful. I'll give the police a buzz to see if they still want to come and talk to you, okay?"

In reply, Danny silently nodded.

The police came around the next morning, and Danny told them all he could remember. They asked Jess some questions about the research too, although they didn't seem to understand how something that happened such a long time ago would impact on anyone now.

Jess was careful what she told them. She felt guilty about not saying more, but she didn't want to tell them what she'd found out about Peter Anderson and his relationship to Sir Robert. She couldn't, even though she was beginning to have strong suspicions that Sir Robert had been behind her dad's attack.

The police left, saying they'd look into the *Aliciana* to see if they could find any links. Jess thought that even if they did find something, at least she wouldn't be the one turning Lukas' grandfather in.

21

Kyra couldn't believe the things she was finding out about Andersson Global's founder, Per Andersson. When Fran had asked her to help her friend Jess with her research, she hadn't considered she was going to be uncovering something as interesting and shocking as the information she had found so far.

Through her own research, she'd managed to find out that Per Andersson's background wasn't quite what everyone had imagined. She had also found definite proof that Per was part of the crew on the *Aliciana*, although under the anglicised name of Peter Anderson. Her contact in Sweden, Nils Berg, had found more information about where Per was born, that he had left Sweden in a great hurry, and that he'd started working on merchant ships – all a great step forward in their research. The start of his working life obviously hadn't been auspicious.

Now, she had to find a way to prove that Per was actually in some way responsible for the sinking. It seemed incredible to her this information had remained hidden for so long. But then, not everyone had the luck to be visited by a ghost from the past. She smiled to herself. Few people, including those who worked with her, would believe that part, anyway.

If Nils could find any more information, she was sure it would certainly paint Per in a less than positive light. But, having had the conversation about the difficulty of tracing records before the First World War, she wasn't sure they would actually find anything.

While researching articles about Sweden during the First World War, Kyra had read about how, although the country was neutral, they'd still supported Germany. It seemed this was mainly because they shared an enemy: Russia, which was an ally of France and Britain at that time. She read that the Swedish intelligence service had employed agents, who during their travels, would report back observations about seaports and other useful information to Germany.

Wondering if there would still be archives, Kyra decided to give Nils a buzz. She rang his number.

"Hej, hej," Nils' deep voice answered.

"Hi, Nils. It's me again. How are you doing?"

"Good. You?"

"Yeah. Are you incredibly busy at the moment, or could I ask you to do a little more searching for me? I know I already owe you, but—"

"Big time!" Nils interrupted. "I'm still waiting to hear how you're going to repay me for my time, Kyra."

Kyra smiled to herself, remembering the tall, blond, God-like hunk that he was. She could think of several ways she'd like to repay Nils, but she wasn't sure if he was still single.

"Mm, we'll talk about that later. So, basically, I'm still trying to find information about Per Andersson. We've had some second-hand information here that he was involved in something quite drastic during World War 1. I think he was some sort of informer. How easy would it be for you to see if there is anything in Swedish archives from that time?"

Nils was quiet for a moment, like he was considering if he had time or even wanted to do more research.

"For you, anything." He laughed. "Seriously, I can see what there is in the archives for World War 1. I remember reading somewhere about reconnaissance agents during that time too. Maybe he was one. You never know, they might have the names of people who worked for the intelligence service then. Yes, I'll have a look, but it may take a little time."

"Nils, that's amazing. Thank you. Take your time. If you find anything, then I'm coming over to celebrate with you. That's a threat."

Laughing at his end of the phone, he said, "That'd better be a promise. I'll get back to you as soon as I've found anything. *Hejdå.*"

Kyra smiled to herself. She definitely looked forward to meeting up with Nils again. They had originally met at a conference not long after they'd both finished their respective university courses. They'd had a fling that had been one of the most enjoyable Kyra had ever had. She'd been sorry when the conference finished and he went back to Sweden. They'd kept in touch but hadn't managed to get together again. Maybe, this might bring them together again.

A few weeks later, Nils contacted Kyra with what he'd found. She was stunned and knew he must have spent some time researching the material. He definitely deserved a congratulatory visit.

Incredibly, Nils found out that Per had killed the Jewish boy back in Vaxholm, when he was 16, which was why he had gone to sea. He had also managed to find some actual documents containing Per's name in the Swedish war archives, and he'd even found information in the German archives too. Everything he'd found proved that Per Andersson was a killer in his youth and that he'd also been responsible for the deaths of everyone who'd drowned on the *Aliciana*, because he didn't pass on the vital information about the German U-boat.

Kyra thanked Nils and told him that as soon as they both had the same weekend free, she'd fly over to visit and would thank him in person. She also told him that when she got around to writing about all of this, he would be credited with his part in the research.

Pleased she'd been able to help Jess, she emailed the information over to her.

22

LLANEIRW, MARCH 2019

Danny grew stronger by the day, and Jess began to feel the closeness they'd always had before her mum's accident returning. Although he was much improved, he wasn't completely back to his full strength, which meant she had to care for him. They spent each and every day together. Jess was nervous about leaving him alone.

However, one afternoon while her dad was having his daily nap, which she understood was part of his recovery, she wandered over to the church to put some fresh flowers on Amy's grave. Over the last few weeks, the back garden, which Danny kept telling her was the next project, had become full of daffodils and tulips and other spring flowers, pushing their way through the undergrowth. Jess cut a selection of them to take to the graveyard.

After clearing the dead flowers and replacing them with the new, Jess sat down on the bench, pulling her hood up to keep herself warm. Although it was a beautiful bright day, there was still a cold wind coming in from the sea. She hugged her coat around her and for a moment shut her eyes. Before she'd even opened them, Jess could feel Amy's presence.

Amy was sitting beside her, smiling.

Thank you. They're beautiful.

Jess smiled back. "I've not seen you for some time. I was beginning to think you'd left me." She quickly got her phone out of her pocket and held it in front of her, thinking that if someone saw her talking to herself, at least with her phone, they would assume she was having a phone conversation.

You've had a lot of things going on. It's good to see your dad is making a recovery. Amy paused. *I'm sorry he got hurt because of what you are doing for me.*

"It's not your fault. I have found things that people didn't want uncovering. But, he's okay, and he is making a good recovery."

They sat quietly together, Jess listening to the sound of the waves washing against the pebble beach and the traffic's continual hum on the expressway.

"I'm pretty certain I know who killed Will, and I'm also sure that soon I'll have actual proof that Peter Anderson was the killer. Once I have that information, then I can make it public, and people will know the truth about the *Aliciana*. And more importantly, hopefully, you and Will will be together at last."

Jess heard Amy sigh.

I will be forever grateful, Jess. In my heart, I still have the flush of first love, which I've clung to for all these years, with an ardent desire for the man I love. I was heartbroken when he died and more so when I couldn't find him on the other side. I had expected to be with him at last. Then, of course, I had to wait to find someone who would hear me.

Amy looked at Jess in a way that reminded Jess of how her mum looked at her when they were having what they both called a 'schmaltzy' moment.

We didn't have enough years together, and with every part of my being, I hate Peter Anderson for taking away that chance we had of building a life together. And for causing the death of my unborn child. There are some things that can never be forgiven.

Jess' heart filled with Amy's sadness. Ever since that first dream, it was as though she channelled Amy's emotions too.

"I promise, I'll do my best to bring you together, Amy."

Standing up, Jess pulled her coat around her again, and walked out of the churchyard, back to see if Danny was still sleeping.

~

A couple of weeks later, Danny was recovering so well he had begun taking short runs along the beach path to build up his stamina. Jess was the happiest she had felt in ages, because their relationship was back on an even keel, and there was much more laughter in the house.

Even the house had a more inviting atmosphere, and as Jess looked around the room where they were both sitting, drinking coffee, the difference compared to when they'd moved in was incredible. The room was warm and inviting and, more than anything, loved. Only one thing was nagging in her mind. She still hadn't heard from Kyra with any more information about Peter.

As if on cue, later that evening an email arrived in Jess' inbox from Kyra. She had actually found all the proof they needed! *Her Swedish contact must be incredible,* Jess thought. They'd done an amazing job, searching the archives.

Jess had tried not to talk about the research since her dad's attack. She had often felt guilty because if she'd listened to him and had allowed Sally to do a spiritual cleanse on the house, none of this would have happened. But Danny had never blamed her at all, so perhaps this was something worth sharing with him.

The next morning over breakfast, Jess told Danny that Kyra's contact had found documents that proved incontrovertibly that Peter Anderson was responsible. Danny was as stunned as she was by the shocking truth. He was even more astonished when Jess told him that she believed it proved that Lukas' grandfather, Sir Robert, had been the one to send the two thugs to their house.

After letting it sink in, Danny asked, "Does Lukas know they were his grandfather's men?"

"I'm not sure. I have a feeling he was questioning his grandfather, but I don't think he knew for sure. Plus, he couldn't accept it was his great-grandad until he had actual proof. He couldn't believe I had seen him in a dream."

"Is that why you've not seen so much of each other?"

"Mostly, yes. But you remember, I told you he came over when you were in hospital?

"Vaguely. He cares for you, Jess. I can see it in his eyes. But, you can't blame him for not believing in ghosts – I mean, I didn't either. And even now, I'm still not totally accepting that it's real."

"I know. I'm going to ring him and see if he can come over. I think it must be hard for him to accept his family were involved. Can you imagine how we'd feel if someone suddenly told us that your great-grandfather had killed people?"

"My great-grandfather wouldn't have managed it in a million years. He was always too drunk." Danny gave a sardonic laugh at the thought.

"You've never told me that before. I can see I'll have to ask you about our ancestors sometime." Jess gave him a hug, and rather than let go of her, he held on to her for a while longer.

"I'm so grateful for you, and proud of you. You know that, don't you?"

"Aw, Dad. Don't be so soppy." She kissed him and pushed him away. "I'm going to give Lukas a ring."

Jess ran upstairs so she could talk to Lukas in private.

Our girl's really growing, Danny said into the air. He couldn't believe how well Jess had coped during the last few months. After losing Kate, their whole world had come to an end. And to make matters worse, he and Jess hadn't been communicating well at all. But he realised, maybe, the 'woo-woo' stuff had, in the long term, brought them closer. Somehow it seemed to have helped Jess, though Danny didn't understand how the hell it could have, considering the horrific dreams she'd experienced.

What he did know was that he was incredibly proud of the young woman Jess was becoming, which also made him sad that Kate wasn't here to see her too. A tear ran down his cheek. God, he missed Kate so much.

Danny's musings were interrupted as Jess rushed back into the room with a grin like the Cheshire cat.

"I guess Lukas is coming down?"

"Yes. I didn't tell him much, just that I had corroborating information about my dreams. He is willing to come and listen, and he didn't sound at all angry. He said he's looking forward to seeing me." Jess couldn't wait to see Lukas, but she also knew that it wouldn't be easy telling him about his great-grandfather's involvement in the disaster.

"When is he arriving?" Danny asked. "We need to tidy the place up a bit."

"What are you saying, Dad? Hasn't my housework been up to your standard?"

"Mm, it's been okay. But from what I've now learnt about Lukas' family, he'll be used to a little more finesse than we have."

"Dad, he's a boy, and he's at uni. Do you think he really cares?" Jess laughed. "He'll be here in the morning."

The last time Lukas had been to the house was when Danny had first gone into hospital, so things had been a bit hectic. Jess didn't even think he'd noticed all the work Danny had done, so she wanted to make everywhere look good, to show off his handiwork. She also wanted to tidy up her room, in case they got any together-time, though she didn't expect much, as Danny would still be around. She berated herself as soon as she had that thought. A few weeks ago, she was worried he wouldn't be around at all, so how could she want him out of the way? But she knew exactly why. Though if Lukas didn't take her news well, she might blow any chance of them ever getting together.

23

Jess could hardly sleep that night. She dreamt that Lukas was so angry he walked out and refused to believe what she was saying, even though she had proof. She ran after him, begging him, but he still ran out, telling her she would never be the person to ruin his family business, and he didn't ever want to see her again.

She woke up and hoped her dream wasn't a bad omen.

Lukas arrived around 11.00 a.m. Jess heard his car, and although she wanted to rush out to meet him, she slowed herself down and nonchalantly ambled along the path.

The first thing he asked was "How is Danny?"

No questions about what she knew. Relieved, Jess related how well her dad had recovered, and led the way back into the house.

"Good to see you're okay, Mr Graham." Lukas shook Danny's hand.

"I told you before, 'Danny', please. I thought we'd go to the pub for lunch, and then you can have the afternoon to chat."

"Sounds good." Lukas smiled at them both.

"Jess, why don't you show Lukas what we've done, now the place looks tidier. I'll make us some coffee."

Jess led Lukas upstairs to show him the changes they'd made, which weren't so many, as it was mostly the ground floor where Danny had finished the makeover.

Lukas smiled when Jess showed him the main bathroom. "I'm so glad you got rid of that awful green bathroom. That was a complete design travesty!"

"Tell me about it. Now, when I walk through the door, it feels like I'm in a hotel, rather than taking a trip back in time."

"Your dad has done a great job, and the new layout downstairs is good too. Did you know he was this good at renovations?"

"He did a few things in our old house, when..." Jess still tripped over any words referring to her mum. "When Mum was alive," she continued. "The reason he moved into this house was because it needed renovating, but mainly it would keep him occupied. And it has, mostly."

Danny interrupted what might have become an awkward silence by shouting, "Coffee's ready."

Over coffee, Jess and Danny asked Lukas about his latest trip to Sweden. He told them all about it, including sharing some of the photos. Jess tried not to show her jealousy when she saw him with a girl. She was as tall as Lukas, and had beautiful long, white-blonde hair with blue eyes, like his. In fact, she was quite similar to Lukas. *Maybe he prefers Swedish blondes,* she thought, twisting her own dark hair.

Unable to contain herself, she asked, "She's pretty. Who is she?"

"That's my sister, Charlott. You think she's pretty?" He grimaced, then smiled. "Yes, she is. We get on well, and it was great that she was out there at the same time as me."

"It's good having a sibling that you get on with. Kate and I couldn't have any more children after we had Jess, which put more pressure on her, especially this last year, but she was all we needed."

"Dad!" Jess flashed him the 'you're embarrassing me' look. Why on earth did parents have to do that? It wasn't even as if she was a teenager. "I'm a young woman, not a kid anymore."

"I know, but sometimes we were disappointed that you didn't have brothers or sisters, and hearing Lukas talk about his sister just made me think about it."

Trying to change the subject and the mood that was making her feel uncomfortable, Jess said they ought to go to the pub.

Full to busting, the three of them were glad the walk back home wasn't far. Danny told them he was going out for a good long trek to walk the meal off and winked at Jess as he left the room. She hoped Lukas hadn't noticed, and was pleased to see he was grabbing something from his bag.

"I bought this for you." Lukas handed her a small, long, thin parcel. "I wanted to apologise to you for rushing off when your... When Danny was so ill."

Jess took it from him, surprised that he'd thought about her at all while he was away.

"You don't need to apologise. Thank you, I didn't expect a gift."

"It's nothing expensive, but it is a traditional bracelet made by the Sami."

Jess tore off the wrapping and opened the box. Inside was a thin red-leather bracelet with a woven braid pattern and a cute little button as the fastening. She put it on her wrist.

"Thank you, it's really cool." She stretched up to kiss him on the cheek. "Who are the Sami?"

"They're the indigenous people of Sweden and the northernmost parts of Finland and Norway. I don't know a lot about the jewellery, but I do know that the leather and the little button both come from caribou. The button is carved from their antlers."

"Wow, that makes it even more special." Jess smiled up at him. She was putting off talking about the main reason he had come – what was now the elephant in the room.

Deciding to just go for it, she said, "There is no easy way to tell you about your great-grandfather, so, do you just want me to show you the information that Kyra found?"

"Yeah."

"It's on my laptop in my room." She led the way back up to her room, and while Lukas sat on her bed, Jess opened up her laptop, found the email from Kyra, and handed the computer over to Lukas for him to read it.

While he was reading, in silence, Jess looked out of the window at the sea, fiddling with her new bracelet, uncertain about how Lukas might react.

After a while, she heard him sigh. Turning around, she saw that Lukas had laid her laptop down on the bed, and with his eyes closed and head down, he was quiet. She knew he was feeling anything but calm. His fists were clenched, and his shoulders were up around his ears.

"I'm sorry, Lukas..."

Lukas looked up at her. "No, I'm sorry. I had my suspicions after we'd been to visit my grandfather. His reactions to a conversation I had with him weren't right. I didn't know why, but I knew in my heart that he was hiding something. And when Danny was beaten up, I was so upset and guilty, because I knew deep down that he was involved. He was the only person I'd told about your interest in the *Aliciana*. How could I have been so blind?"

He looked near to tears. Jess sat beside him on the bed and

hugged him.

"You couldn't have been sure, but even then, it's not something you expect to hear about your own grandfather, is it?"

"But I should have told my dad and got him to talk to my grandfather, rather than try to ignore my worries. And, I was so horrible to you about your dreams, and how they were affecting you. Can you forgive me, Jess?"

Still hugging him, she moved back so she could see his face. "Lukas, you know I can."

She didn't mean to, but unable to help herself, she kissed him. Not a friendly, quick kiss, but a long, deep kiss, to which Lukas responded.

Jess stood up and moved the laptop from her bed and shut the door. Turning back towards Lukas, she took off the T-shirt she was wearing and knelt in front of him.

"I've been wanting to do this for so long," she said before continuing to kiss him passionately.

Between kisses and undressing each other, Lukas asked, "What about your dad?"

"Don't worry, he's out, and even if he comes back, he won't come in my room. Plus, I think he's got someone who he is seeing too, so he won't be back yet."

They both stripped off, and all the pent-up emotion and lust that had been building up, lurking behind the unsettled friendship, broke free in a passionate act of lovemaking that left them both gasping and happily satisfied.

Lukas traced the shape of Jess' face with his fingers as they gazed into each other's eyes. "I should have done that ages ago, but I wasn't sure when it would be the right time."

"Seriously, didn't I tell you last time you were here how much I wanted you?"

"You said you didn't want comfort sex. Isn't that just what you gave me?" Lukas asked.

"Cheeky. If that was comfort sex, then we'd better try again and make it less comfortable." Jess pushed Lukas onto his back and began kissing him, moving down his body. Very quickly, he grabbed her and they made love again, their bodies totally in sync with one another's.

Danny walked back into the house and found Lukas and Jess downstairs, making coffee and working their way through a pack of chocolate biscuits.

"Good to see you two are still talking. I was worried that doors might have been slammed again."

"No, everything is fine, Dad."

"More than fine, Danny."

The look that passed between the pair of them told Danny more than any of their words did. He knew they'd made up.

"So, what's going to happen next?" he asked them both.

"I'm going to talk to my dad, show him the email info that Jess has forwarded to me, and he'll make decisions about what to do next. Knowing my dad, he'll definitely do the right thing," Lukas answered, then said tentatively, "I'm really sorry about your beating, Danny. I now know it was Grandfather who organised it. I had my suspicions, but couldn't believe it. I should have done, so I'm sorry."

"Lukas, lad. It wasn't you that did it, and anyone would find it hard to believe that of their relatives, so don't worry. I'm fine now, and luckily, with no long-term after-effects. Please don't apologise. So, what are you two going to do tonight? You are staying again tonight, aren't you, Lukas?"

"Thanks, yes. Jess has organised to meet up with Fran and some other friends at the pub tonight."

"Oh, that's living it up. The highlife of Llaneirw." Danny laughed.

Later, on their return from the pub, Lukas sneaked into Jess' room so they could spend at least one night together. They knew they probably wouldn't see each other for a couple of weeks, at least, because once the news hit about his great-grandfather, he suspected the life of his family would become front-page news.

While Lukas and Jess slept, Amy stood watching. She was grateful to Jess for finding the truth, but sad that the boy she loved was related to Will's killer. Unlike most couples, she and Will had never had the luxury of getting bored with each other or taking each other for granted. Their promise of years together had been snatched away, and now Amy was more confident than she had ever been in the last sixty years that soon she would be with her soulmate once again.

She knew this was probably the last time she'd be inside her house, and she glanced down at Jess with a look of love and contentment. For the first time in decades, there was a calmness and serenity around her, which she'd not experienced since first meeting Will and being gifted his love. It was all thanks to this young woman, who she'd watched grow over these many months. Amy could no longer feel the terrible grief that had surrounded Jess when they first met, and she recognised that, in some small way, she'd helped her, hopefully more than she'd upset her. Amy ran her hand over Jess' hair, which lifted very gently, like a soft blowing zephyr, and for the last time, she disappeared into the shadows of the house.

24
ANGLESEY, APRIL 2019

Robert had just poured himself a drink when he heard the doorbell, and seconds later, James barged into the room, not waiting for Delyth to open the study door.

"What did you think you were doing, Dad?" James demanded.

Robert turned to Delyth and waved her away, telling her to close the door on the way out. "Hello, son. I wasn't expecting to see you tonight. What are you on about?" Robert asked, although he had an inkling of exactly what he was talking about.

"To start with, Lukas has come to me saying that his friend's dad has been attacked by some heavies and that she's been told to 'back off' researching into the *Aliciana* – basically, Anderson family affairs. Her father was in hospital with head injuries," James said.

Robert sauntered across the room towards the fireplace, where James was standing. He worked hard on looking aloof, and even now in his mid-seventies, he knew his appearance helped him maintain that impression. He always dressed smartly. Today, he was wearing slacks and a branded sailing jumper and shirt; the epitome of an elderly, wealthy man.

Leaning against the fireplace, Robert answered in a matter-of-fact tone. "I didn't want them sullying our family name."

"You don't think you did that yourself, by sending your goons after this family? What the hell did you think you were doing?"

"There are things that could be made public," Robert said.

"Dad, things are already going to come out. What could be worse?" James asked. "You are lucky that he hasn't been able to give the police any descriptions or information."

"So how come you know it was me?" He'd given himself away. But before James could answer, as an afterthought, Robert added, "Anyway, he was told that if he continued to search, we'd hurt his daughter."

"You what? More to the point, how the heck do you know these people? You sound like a gangster." It seemed James couldn't believe what he was hearing. "Lukas was right. You've gone completely mad."

His words hung in the air. Robert took a drink of the whisky he'd poured when James burst in. "Firstly, I'm no gangster, I just happen to know a few men who have helped me out over the years." He took another sip of his whisky, then continued. "But there is something more I need to tell you."

Sir Robert sat down heavily in one of the leather armchairs by the fire. "Some years ago, while clearing out his belongings, I found some disturbing information about my father," he said. "Actually, incriminating information." He looked up at his son with an expression James had never seen on his father's face before. Shame. This, a man who never apologised for anything.

"For God's sake, what can be worse than me finding out that you send people to rough-up anyone who you don't like?" James asked.

Robert let out a sigh. "I found some evidence among my dad's things that suggested he was working for Germany during the war."

James kept quiet. He already knew this but was shocked that his father had always known. He played along. "He was a German spy?" James laughed. "Come on, really?"

The silence that followed was uncomfortable. Robert sensed that his words had troubled James.

He had no intention of owning up that he already knew his grandfather was a spy, so he asked, "What on earth did you find?"

Robert took another long drink of his whisky. "A letter from the German consulate in Sweden, thanking him for his part in sinking the *Aliciana*. I couldn't afford for anyone to find that information. Think what it would do to the company, James. No one else apart from you and me need to know about Dad's German links. That's the whole reason I was trying to stop them researching."

Father and son glared at one another.

"What did you do with the letter? Did you keep it?" James asked.

"No, of course not. I burnt it, there and then. I didn't want anyone finding it after I died."

"As if your nefarious actions haven't harmed the company enough," James said. "This information, plus the information Lukas' friend has, will sink us." James went over to his father's drinks cabinet and poured himself a substantial whisky too, taking a large gulp before continuing. "I already knew he'd been working for the Germans, and I also have proof that he was involved in the sinking."

Robert stared at James. "How do you know that? How can it be proved? Everyone's dead!"

"Yes, everyone is dead, thanks to your father." James began

pacing backwards and forwards. "Do you know how many people died on that ship?" But before Robert could answer, he continued. "I have a letter written in 1944 by a friend of grandfather's, called Hobson Ward. Even without your information, this, plus spending time searching documents in Sweden and the German consulate archives, anyone with a bit of nous could find the truth."

Robert was slightly rattled, though he was still not ready to accept defeat. He hadn't spent all of these years building up the company his father had started to let some silly scandal from the First World War ruin their reputations now. "Seriously, James? A letter can easily disappear, and why would anyone want to search documents? Well, not anymore. No one needs to hear about it. Don't be so naïve, James."

His son was clearly livid. "Naïve! I am questioning everything I knew about my family. In the last few days, I've learnt that not only is my own father a bully, but that my grandfather was a killer, and he was anti-Semitic, which I shouldn't actually have been surprised about. I always noticed how very quiet you were when there was any discussion about the Jews. Haven't you always wondered why I kept Charlott and Lukas away from you?"

Robert interrupted. "After Dad died, I was very careful to keep my views to myself. I would never have shared them with the children."

"Mother wouldn't have let you," said James.

Robert took another drink. "You know I had a very strict upbringing with Dad, living with his outdated Lutheran beliefs, which had been handed down from his father." He paused to drain the last drop of whisky from his glass. "If he hadn't started the company, I think he might have gone off the rails, to be honest."

James continued. "He'd already gone off the rails, for God's sake. And neither his nor your upbringing is any excuse. There is also evidence that the Admiralty sent a warning message to the ship, warning that there were U-boats in the area, but they didn't get the message, because, as we now know, radio operator Anderson destroyed it!" His voice had crescendoed as he spoke the last two words. "And then he had the gall to put himself into the position of being a hero."

"But we can still keep all of this quiet. Nobody needs to know," Robert said now, with far less bluster.

"You silly old fool! Who do you think you are? We're not above justice, just because you have the money to pay heavies to scare people off. With the amount of information these people researching Peter have found and will continue to find, there will be plenty of proof," James replied. He finished the rest of his whisky in one go. "I don't expect to hear about any more threats made to Jess and Danny Graham in the future. If I do, I will be turning you in to the police myself."

James stood to leave. Walking out of the room, he said, "Now I need to find a way to take care of the collateral damage you and my grandfather have caused this family and our company. And I need to apologise to Mr Graham."

Robert remained sitting in his armchair, staring at the door his son had just slammed shut behind him, as, for the first time in his life, the consequences of his and his father's actions began to sink in.

25

The *Helena* was Sir Robert's pride and joy, although even when she was alive, Helena wasn't that keen to go out on the sea in the vessel named after her, at least not in the UK. She didn't mind so much when they had spent time sailing out in the Caribbean, where the sea was generally calm, and a beautiful blue, compared to the dark, cold sea of home. Robert had surprised her by buying a yacht manufactured in Sweden, particularly as he rarely wanted to be linked to anything Swedish. Yet he'd been adamant that he wanted the best, and Hallberg–Rassy were certainly one of the best yacht makers in the world.

A few days after James had visited and abruptly left his house, Sir Robert had received a short, angry phone call from him telling him that he had been given the irrefutable, written proof from the German archives that Per Andersson had been in the pay of the German military.

Robert had been unable to believe that someone had managed to find this information after all of these years. Feeling unsettled and completely out of sorts, he'd decided to take the

Helena out for a sail. He wanted to breathe in the sea air and feel the wind blowing in his face. He knew it would calm him down and settle his worries about his father's past being raked up. He collected his sailing gear, and after packing it in his car, told Delyth he probably wouldn't get home for supper but would eat at the sailing club in Cemaes.

The weather forecast had been good, and with the wind behind him, the *Helena* was soon gliding over the waves. Sir Robert loved being on the water, the wind blowing through his hair, spray occasionally washing over his face. He was in his element. Sailing westwards of Cemaes, he was aiming to head out to sea on the northern side of The Skerries islets and lighthouse. In fact, this had been the lighthouse that had raised the alarm when the *Aliciana* was torpedoed in 1915. He often sailed in this area, knowing his father had sailed here before him. He glanced at the lighthouse as he sailed past it on his port side. Eventually, no land was visible at all. Robert felt invincible in control of his vessel, as he had always been throughout every aspect of his life. He was used to being in control.

However, about twenty minutes later, he was aware that the wind had shifted, and he was being thrown around by the waves as an unexpected squall appeared from nowhere.

Hanging on to the helm to keep the boat heading into the wind, he had no chance to shorten sail and the force of the squall on his full sails threatened to capsize the boat at any moment.

Amid the churning waves, Robert suddenly noticed a cardinal mark. He experienced a sharp and unwelcome pang of fear. He knew cardinal markers were to indicate the position of an underwater danger. Surely the wind hadn't blown him so far out that he was close to the sunken *Aliciana*?

Sir Robert continued to hang on for dear life as the growing waves swept over the deck. He was tiring. He wasn't as young or as strong as he used to be, and he was finding it harder to remain upright as his sea-legs also appeared to be failing him. He was desperately trying to stay on the boat but was swallowing far more seawater than was healthy.

Finally, his strength gave out as the boat broached and dipped under a huge wave that lashed across the beam and pounded the deck, washing him over the side. As he fell, he hit his head, not enough to knock him out, but enough to disorientate him.

Sir Robert thrashed around, the control he had been bragging about to himself completely gone. Frantically, he kept looking around for his boat so he could get back on board. His life jacket was keeping him afloat, but his energy was disappearing. Each time any waves pushed him onto his front, he swallowed mouthfuls of water before the life jacket turned him onto his back. This was his worst nightmare; his boat had disappeared from his view.

His energy was waning, and then he felt something pulling him down. He tried to shake it off, whatever it was. Maybe he'd got caught up in something from the yacht that had also fallen into the water, and as he was battling to free himself, he looked around in panic to see what was stopping him from surfacing completely. To his horror, emerging from the churning darkness of the sea beneath him, he could see pale, skeletal hands reaching up for him, grabbing onto his legs, his arms and finally his torso. The more he struggled, the more the phantoms clung onto him with far greater strength.

Sir Robert began to scream and, in doing so, swallowed mouthfuls of seawater. The water began to fill his lungs; the ghostly beings began to win. Unable to fight any longer, he was dragged lower and lower, into the fathoms of darkness beneath. As life began to leave his body, he heard the words: "The sins of the father..."

The *Helena* slowly recovered from the broach, its sails in shreds, its helm swinging back and forwards as though greeting the calmer seas ahead.

26

LLANEIRW, APRIL 2019

Having a shower before bed, Jess had found herself singing, something she hadn't done since moving to Llaneirw. She recognised that her entire mood had been more upbeat in the last few days. Of course, there were several reasons for this. She and Lukas were now an 'item', as Fran would say, and the house had a new lightness about it, as though a shroud had been lifted. It was something she couldn't quite explain, but she knew it was more than the renovations her dad had done. Earlier in the evening, she'd spoken to Lukas, who had already had a heated conversation with his father about his grandfather's part in the sinking of the Aliciana. Jess and Lukas had also arranged to meet up the following weekend in Manchester. All was well in the world.

As Jess walked into the bedroom, instantly, the atmosphere changed. She knew Amy was present, though she couldn't see her anywhere.

In her head, Jess heard Amy's voice. *Jess, look out of the window, towards the church.*

Doing as she was told, Jess opened one of her curtains and looked over to the church. She gasped. Standing in a pool of light created by the lantern above the lychgate were Will and Amy. They were arm in arm, both looking as they would when they were last together as newlyweds. Incredibly, somehow, the light also shone into Jess' room. Together, Will and Amy looked up at her room, and when they saw her at the window, as one, they lifted their hands and waved. Inside her head, she heard two voices say, *Thank you.* As she remained watching, they turned. As they did so, an intense, brighter light filled the gateway and also illuminated her room. Amy and Will walked into the light, then were suddenly gone. The light disappeared, and the churchyard was empty once more. Her room also returned to being lit only by her bedside light.

At that moment, Jess experienced a feeling of profound loss, though not grief. It was more as though a heaviness from deep within had been lifted. Into the air, Jess whispered, "Goodbye."

The following morning, Jess bounded down the stairs to join Danny, who was making breakfast.

"You sound like a charge of bulls coming down the stairs," he said.

"I can't help it. I'm feeling happy and bright this morning. Look at the sun. It's going to be lovely today."

Danny glanced at her. "Are you the same girl I've been living with for the last few months?"

"Ha, ha! I had the most wonderful sleep last night, and...I saw Amy and Will. Together."

Danny looked at her again. "You saw them together! Does that mean? Er, what does that mean?" He laughed.

"It means, now they know exactly what happened, Will and Amy are on the same plane, and last night I saw them walk into the churchyard together and disappear into the light. They looked so happy together."

"Does that mean we no longer have a spirit in the house?" Danny asked.

"Yes, it does, although you don't have to sound quite so happy about it, Dad. Amy and Will are reunited, because you, me, Fran and Kyra helped them." She gave him a hug and clung onto him for some time.

"I'm glad you didn't let me persuade Sally to come and do a cleansing thing. Even though I hated seeing you so hurt at times, it's all worked out."

"Let's have a celebratory breakfast, and later, we can celebrate over a good meal."

Danny turned the TV on so he could watch the morning news programmes while they ate their breakfast. He stopped eating. "Isn't that Lukas' dad?" He recognised him from the day he'd turned up with a bottle of expensive whisky and an apology.

Jess looked up at the screen, chewing a mouthful of bacon. "Mm. Turn it up."

They caught the end of something, and then the news presenter in the TV studio said, "We're going over to Angela Bryant, who is talking to James Anderson, MBE and CEO of Andersson Global. Angela..."

"Thank you, Fergal. I'm outside Andersson Global Headquarters in Manchester, where James Anderson has just arrived." Blocking his way into the building, she shoved a microphone in front of James. "Mr Anderson, have you got time to talk to us, please?"

James looked harassed, and as if he hadn't slept the night before. Before waiting for him to answer, she continued. "Mr Anderson, we are very sorry to hear of the death of Sir Robert last night."

Danny and Jess looked at each other in disbelief.

"Is it right that Sir Robert's yacht went down off the coast of Anglesey, in the same vicinity where the *Aliciana* sank in 1915?"

James cleared his throat. "As far as we know, yes. We don't know what the problem was, but his empty yacht was found yesterday, and after a long search, no body was found, so he is presumed dead."

"Mr Anderson, do you have any comment about the allegations that your grandfather, Peter Anderson, was a German spy?"

Again, Angela Bryant shoved the microphone in front of James, in expectation of an answer.

Jess and Danny watched James steel himself to give his answer. He took his time and eventually said, "All I will say at this moment is that we have uncovered some disturbing news about my grandfather, and I will be giving a detailed press conference later in the week after we've had time to process my father's death. I'd ask you to give my family and me some space over the next few days to grieve in peace. Thank you."

James turned and started to walk inside the building.

The newswoman shouted after him. "Will you be apologising to the surviving family members of the sinking of the *Aliciana*?"

Without turning, or flinching, James disappeared through the main entrance of Andersson Global.

The newswoman spoke to camera.

"At the present time, we don't know if this was a tragic accident or if Sir Robert took his own life, following the allegations of his father's part in the sinking of the *Aliciana*, and the huge loss of life which ensued. Back to Fergal in the studio."

Fergal thanked Angela Bryant and moved on to the next story.

Danny turned the sound down on the TV and looked up at Jess. She had tears streaming down her face. He was about to say something, when she said, 'Don't worry, Dad, these are happy tears. Amy and Will can finally rest. The truth is going to be made public, and families can at last hold someone responsible." Jess let out a long, calming sigh. "Now we can get on with our lives. Even Lukas' family will put this behind them. James is nothing like his father or grandfather."

"I'm just glad to have my girl back, and it appears the sea has taken its revenge." Danny waved his hands in front of him. "Wooooo."

"Don't be so dramatic, Dad!"

27
LETTER TO KATE, 2022

Kate, I needed to write this to you. I read somewhere that writing a letter is the best way to release feelings and emotions. If you are watching over us, you may know all of this already. However, even though Jess and I have lived through some strange 'woo-woo' stuff, I'm still on the fence when it comes to completely believing, myself. After you tragically left us, I didn't want to live in this world without you, Kate. And if it hadn't been for Jess, I might have done something stupid. I'm pretty sure I'd have hunted down that stupid cocky little sod that took you from me and ended his life too. Luckily for me, Jess needed me.

Initially I was sure I'd made a huge mistake in moving to Llaneirw, but despite our spiritual visitations, and Jess becoming a sleuth for a ghost – things turned out pretty well.

In a strange way, the odd relationship Jess had with Amy ultimately helped her to overcome her grief. She had something else to focus on.

For a long time, we barely existed, hardly communicating, but thankfully, Jess and I are back to where we were before your accident, and if anything, our relationship is even stronger. She has matured into an amazing young woman. You'd be so proud of her, Kate, and I think she looks more and more like you each day.

Following Sir Robert's death, his son, James, gave a press conference where he apologised to any living family members of the *Aliciana* sinking. He set up a memorial fund linked to a charity. From the moment he took over as the company's CEO, he developed the philanthropic side of the business, and the way he dealt with what could have ruined many other businesses was admirable. He also gave Kyra an exclusive interview so that she was able to write a long article that was picked up by several national newspapers, giving her career a great boost. She was a huge help when Jess was researching stuff and got stuck.

Jess finally went to university in late 2019. Once she moved to Manchester, her relationship with Lukas blossomed, and they eventually moved in together. He has a small terraced house in Fallowfield, about three miles from the city centre.

You'd like him, Kate; he's a very clever, bright, and kind young man who loves our girl to bits. Though it was a difficult time for him to accept what his great-grandfather had done, and that it was Jess who had uncovered his betrayal to his country, they supported each other through it. They remind me of us two when we were first together. The flush of young love!

I need to tell you that I've met someone, and during the pandemic, she and I grew closer together. We spent most of lockdown in our own 'bubble'. I think we kept each other sane. I was missing Jess, so much, and of course I

couldn't see her, so Anna, (that's her name), and I became much closer.
Kate, I hope you understand I'm not replacing you in any way. In fact, you remember, we used to talk about wanting each other to 'move on' if something happened to either of us. But, I'm not moving on. You will always be a part of our family. You're part of Jess too, so I can never forget you. And Anna understands and fully accepts that.
I know we'd talked about travelling when Jess left home, to help us overcome 'empty nest' syndrome. Well, I still need that. So, Anna has sold her café, and I've sold this house, and we've bought a larger house in Broad Haven, in Pembrokeshire. We're going to run it as a B & B, and then out-of-season we're going to travel.
When I broke the news to Jess about my relationship with Anna, she took it in her stride, telling me she was glad I wasn't going to be alone.
So here we are, three years on, we're out of the pandemic, with things getting back to normal. A new normal, but life is back on track.
You'll be proud and delighted to hear that despite all the upheaval of the pandemic, and the universities virtually closing, Jess gained her BA degree: a first in geography. Lukas was a year ahead of her, so he is already working for Andersson Global, and I think Jess will join them too. They are both in Sweden at the moment and have been for around six months. They love it, and I wouldn't be surprised if they didn't decide to stay there, although they also have an apartment in Manchester. We'll see.
I just hope you can see that Jess has developed into the beautiful, mature young woman that we always knew she would. And I hope that I have been enough as a parent because it was bloody difficult without you.

The last few years may have been difficult at times for all of us, but the possibilities for the future are amazing.
If I've learnt nothing else, I've come to understand the power of love, and how enduring it can be.
Kate, forever yours – you will always be in my heart.
Danny

AUTHOR NOTE

William Campbell

1883–1915

Amy Campbell

1881–1956

Echoes of Drowning is inspired by the true story of William and Amy Campbell.

When I was growing up, Mum always told me stories about her Uncle Willie (my grandad's brother) and his wife, Amy, who were onboard the HMS Lusitania when it went down on 7th May 1915. Uncle Willie drowned, and his body was never recovered. Aunty Amy lived in Llandudno, just below the Great Orme, so she could see the sea until her death in 1956. She didn't remarry and had no children.

My mum was terrified of the sea, and whether or not stories of Uncle Willie's demise scared her, I don't know. But while doing research, I've found that certain aspects of the stories she told me weren't exactly correct – they probably lost something through retelling, over the years.

I have always been fascinated by Amy and Willie's story and when it came to writing my second novel, I decided I'd write about them. Amy's story is one of enduring love. To have lived by the sea that took her husband for all those years is so poignant.

Not being a historian and because I didn't want to be tied by facts, my story is very loosely based on them (although I do keep their Christian names). My story is set in 2018, and the name of the ship, the reason for the sinking, the site of the sinking and the village where Amy lived alone for all of those years, are all from my imagination.

I did read books (*Dead Wake* by Erik Larson), and researched information about the Lusitania so I would understand how it must have felt to be on the ship when it was sinking, and ultimately sank, with the loss of 1195 lives, including men, women and children.

These two images were among my mum's family photos. Although I know for certain that the man is Uncle Willie, I'm not 100% certain that the lady is Amy. However, a small and very pixelated image from a newspaper at the time (which I was given by the Facebook group, RMS Lusitania Association of Relatives and Researchers) shows a picture of the couple before they got on the ship. The woman in the photo I have is an extremely close match to the one in the newspaper clipping. However, I'm not certain if it is Amy, and there is no one left alive in my family to ask. In writing my book though, this is how I imagined her.

ACKNOWLEDGMENTS

I have many people to thank for helping me with aspects of this book.

Grateful thanks go to:

- all my friends who continue to support me with my writing.
- Pauline, Carolyne, Amanda, Patricia, Thea and Alice for giving their valuable time to read and comment on the book after I'd first completed it.
- Carolyne's husband, John, who helped me with my yacht chapter, as I know absolutely nothing about sailing.
- Jeff Wilson from Tennessee, who I met on Facebook and has been an absolute star, translating timetables, sending me images of the rail-carriages of the time (1911), and explaining the route the train would take.
- Samantha Scott, a friend and Psychic, who talked to me about ghosts, spirits and the type of things that people experience upon meeting them.
- my friend, Edward Barham, who is a walking encyclopaedia when it comes to anything historic. His advice was invaluable, as history is not my strong point.
- my cousin, Mary Fortey who very kindly did some ancestry research for me as she has been researching

my father's side of the family, and was happy to look at my mum's side too.

- the Facebook Group: RMS Lusitania Association of Relatives and Researchers who shared some very helpful research about my relatives.
- Arthur Cole who, as he has previously, provided me with information about police procedure.
- Delyth Woods for help with the Welsh language, and helping me give my village with an appropriate name.
- Charlott McAncsh for help in choosing places in Sweden for my characters to hail from.
- Nick Ruddle who helped me find the clarity in the plot line at the beginning of my writing.
- Claire Cronshaw, my amazing editor.
- Gavin Kemp for his support and help with all things technical.
- Last but not least, to Conrad, my husband, who is my biggest fan!

ALSO BY LIS MCDERMOTT

He is Not Worthy

AUTHOR REQUEST

Hello,
Thank you for taking the time to read **Echoes of Drowning**.

- Rate or review this book on your favourite site.
- Tell your friends.
- Add it to a genre list on Goodreads.
- Connect with the author: friend, follow or like their fan page on Facebook.

Authors work hard to be noticed in the crowded world of books, and often it's word-of-mouth that makes all the difference.

Thank you for your support and help.
Lis McDermott

ABOUT THE AUTHOR

Lis McDermott spent thirty-four years working in music education, latterly as a schools adviser and OFSTED inspector, before leaving education in 2008 to set up her own photography business.

In the 90s, during her time in education, she co-wrote *Nelson Music,* a series of books to support the classroom music curriculum. She published her first solo book in 2014, a photography book called *Headshot Diva: why your business profile affects your bottom line.*

Having awoken another passion, she has now published an autobiography – a book of short stories and four poetry anthologies. She also mentors others to write their books.

Lis lives in Royal Wootton Bassett with her husband Conrad, with whom she shares a love of music and films.

facebook.com/LisMcDermottAuthor

x.com/LisMcDAuthor

instagram.com/lismcdermott

linkedin.com/in/lismcdermott

Printed in Great Britain
by Amazon

41618099R00130